α

Loyalty 2

By: EL Griffin

Shanice

I was on my way to meet up with Silk and I was on edge. I don't know why I was so nervous. Maybe it was the fact that I was finally ready to give him a real chance. All I know was that nigga better have his shit together and not try and play me.

He was telling me I was the only woman he wanted and that there wasn't no other bitches he was fucking with. But the way things turned out last time I let him talk me into some shit left me wondering if he was really being honest with me. I figured since I was leaving for school it would give us some distance from each other so I could see if he was on bullshit or was really serious and capable of keeping his dick in his pants before I let my heart get involved.

We were meeting at the same park that we fucked at the other day. I don't know what came over me to be fucking this nigga out in the middle of a damn park in a car but the sex was so good the first time I couldn't help it. Then his ass persuaded me to go chill back at his house with him until the meeting I set up with Torio, and the sex got even better.

The shit was the best I ever had even though I wasn't about to admit that to his ass since he already had a big head and talked too much shit. If I let him know how his dick game blew my mind I would never hear the end of it with his cocky ass.

While I was at his place we not only spent time fucking but we also got to know each other better. He was easy as hell to talk to and had a good sense of humor. We stayed cracking jokes on each other and talking shit the whole time. We had a good time together and it was nice to feel that connection with him again.

I pulled into a parking spot near the basketball court where there was a game going on. I saw Silk pull up next to me before he stepped out of his car looking good as hell. He walked over to my door and opened it up without waiting for me to. I stepped out and adjusted my clothes before we headed over to the picnic area.

I felt his gaze on me as I walked in front of him and when I turned around of course he was focused on my ass. I shook my head and smiled at him before I turned back around and kept walking. He was a confident nigga who had no shame at all but I didn't mind as long as he kept his attention on me and no other bitch.

I chose to meet up at the park so we would be able to sit down and talk about shit out in the open. That way we wouldn't get sidetracked. I knew if we went back to his place again like he suggested there would be less talking and more fucking. I wanted to have a real ass talk with his ass before we moved forward so he would take what I was saying serious.

"What's up Shanice? You're staring a nigga down is only gonna make me fuck you right out here. So say what's on your mind."

This big headed ass nigga always had one thing on his mind I swear. I got right to the point since looking at him longer and longer was turning me on.

"I'm ready to see where this goes Kenneth, but only if what you've been telling me is the truth. I'm not a weak or dumb bitch. I know you're a nigga who gets around, but if you wanna be with me you have to cut all that shit out and not sling your dick around."

"I ain't never been a one woman nigga shorty."

I started to open my mouth and talk shit but he held up his hand and stopped me. So I let him finish.

"I want you Shanice. I want to be the nigga you need me to be so I'm gonna do that shit for you. I see a future for us. Now are you really ready to be my queen?"

As I listened to the words coming out of his mouth I tried to read if what he was telling me was just some bullshit or if he was being honest. It all sounded good, but I hoped he lived up to the shit he was spitting.

My thoughts were interrupted by the ringing of my cell phone. I forgot Larissa was supposed to call me to tell me about the surprise Money had for her last night. She hated surprises, but when she told me about it yesterday I could tell she was really excited. She was head over heels in love with that nigga.

I went ahead and pulled my phone out to answer it. The conversation with Silk could wait. I was ready to hear all the details from my main bitch. I was surprised when an unfamiliar voice spoke instead of Larissa.

"Hello, I'm trying to reach Ms. Shanice Jenkins," some man who sounded like a salesperson stated.

"This is her." I replied.

"We have a patient. A Larissa McNeil and you were listed as her next of kin."

"Where is she? What happened? I started screaming into the phone as my heart rate sped up.

"I'm afraid I can't share details over the phone. We need you to come to the hospital right away."

After getting the hospital information I hung up the phone and started running towards my car. I needed to catch a flight and see what the fuck was going on with Larissa. I guess Silk followed me because he hopped in the passenger seat of my jeep without saying a word to me. Tears were rolling down my face. Larissa was my damn sister and whatever happened to her was serious enough that she couldn't call me herself. I tried to clear my mind and get my shit together while I drove fast as hell to the airport.

Messiah (Money)

I woke up and felt the cold steel under me. Remembering where the fuck I was, I pushed myself up into a sitting position and leaned back against the wall of the cargo hold I was being kept in. I didn't know exactly how many days had passed. But the roll of the waves from below let me know that the ship was still moving.

Three niggas would bring me a meal what seemed like twice a day and never said shit in the process. There were a few small shop lights lining the sides of the crate wall and my eyes had adjusted to the dim light.

I was in pain from the injuries I suffered from the crash. The mothafuckas untied my legs so I was able to move around a little. But one of my legs was so fucked up that every time I moved sharp pains shot through my entire body. They still had my ass handcuffed so there wasn't shit I could really do but just wait this out and see what the fuck these niggas had planned for me.

I would never go out like a bitch and let another nigga break me no matter what I went through. I fucked up going to that meeting alone in the first place and now I was paying for that shit. I was blind to all of it and too trusting of Fe which is why I ended up getting myself into such a fucked up situation.

I was stuck here now and hoping like hell they hadn't gotten to LaLa. She was my fuckin' heart and I needed to make sure I got back to her and my son she was carrying. Her ass was probably going crazy worrying about me and that was the last thing she needed right now. I didn't want to put her through none of this shit and tried to keep her away from my street life. She was a rider though and right now I needed her to hold shit down until I could get back to her.

It seemed like forever before I was pulled out of the damn cargo hold I was being kept in. Finally the mothafuckas dragged me outside. The light was blinding my eyes so I couldn't even see where the fuck I was. Once my eyes focused and got used to the bright ass sunlight I took in my surroundings and saw I was at a cargo port. It seemed like we were in an even more tropical place than Miami from the hot ass temperature and humidity. Somebody came behind where I was standing and unlocked my handcuffs before stepping around in front of me.

Fe's bitch ass stood there smiling at me like he was the happiest nigga alive. But I knew there was more to this shit. Since he went to all this trouble bringing me to wherever the fuck I was. He fucked up by keeping me alive and didn't even know it yet.

I stood tall with my hands folded in front of me. Even though my body was screaming out in pain I would never let his ass see that shit. I glared right back at the mothafucka with no emotion showing on my face.

He placed the key to the handcuffs in his pocket and folded his arms across his chest while he continued to look at me with his eyebrows raised. It was like he was waiting for me to beg or some shit. He could keep on waiting if that was the case because I wasn't begging for shit from anyone other than God himself.

"We had to take certain precautions so you would understand who you were dealing with." Fe said in his deep ass accent.

I didn't know why the fuck he brought me here or what he wanted me to say but I wasn't a bitch. Even though I was weaker than usual from the shit I had been through over the past few days I made sure to stand up tall and look the mothafucka right in the eyes.

"What the fuck is this shit Fe? You doing all this for a reason. You might as well get to the fucking point!"

"Right you are boy! Welcome to Belize Money." He started laughing like he said some funny shit.

Then he nodded his head before turning to walk away, signaling two of his bodyguards. They roughly grabbed my arms and escorted me behind him. I was pushed into the backseat of a black navigator and the driver began driving us away from the port.

As we rode through the streets of Belize I saw the restaurants, bars, and shops turn into a crowded ass city. The city streets were narrow and filled with people. After driving past what looked like the slums of the city there was more land and the houses got bigger. We kept riding right past all that shit and finally made it to this little ass hut that seemed to be in the middle of fucking nowhere.

I was pulled out of the car and led inside with one of the niggas holding a gun to my back. After stepping inside the little ass shack that was hot as hell the mothafuckas had me sit in a chair. The only thing in the one room house was a table and the chair they had me sitting in. Fe walked through the door while on his phone and I was able to catch the end of the conversation he was having.

"I got the boy. I want it all Emeri. Here."

He handed me the phone, so I took it and held it up to my ear. I heard another nigga's voice who I had never heard before with the same deep accent as Fe. The man on the other line said hello and called me by name.

"Yo." I said once I heard him say my name for the second time.

"Give the phone back to Fe." The man responded back to me.

I went ahead and gave the phone back to his ass. I wasn't sure what the hell was going on yet but it seemed like I was being held hostage or some shit and Fe was trying to get a ransom by having me here.

"Stop yu rass and do what the fuck I said or you'll never see him again."

Whoever the man was that Fe was talking to was making him mad as fuck. He raised his voice and started talking with broken English making it harder to understand what the fuck he was saying. But I wasn't a dumb nigga and knew he was talking about my ass. I wondered who the man was on the other end of the phone call and what the fuck Fe was up to. It was obvious whatever it was had him uneasy by how he was acting and I planned on using that shit to my advantage.

Fe hung up the phone and placed it in the middle of the table. Then he started walking back out of the small house. He stopped at the door and said some shit that surprised the hell out of me.

"You better hope your father comes through or it's your life." Fe said before leaving out.

The mothafuckas left my ass alone in the house after that. There wasn't shit I could really do. I didn't know what the fuck Fe was talking about but I planned to pay attention to every detail and use that shit to get the fuck out of here. There wasn't a doubt in my mind that I would get out of this situation and make it back to LaLa.

The cell phone Fe left on the table worked and could call out. So I picked it up and dialed Larissa's number. I needed to get up with her and let her know I was alive and alright even if that shit wasn't all the way true. I wanted to make sure she wasn't' stressed out since that was all I had been thinking about since I regained consciousness. I called back to back with no answer and started getting worried that something might have happened to her. Maybe she wasn't answering because the call was coming from an unknown number I thought.

The phone didn't have messaging so I decided to call Silk on his personal cell and see if I could at least get up with someone back home. Only a few niggas knew his cell number and we always picked up any calls that came through in case it was an emergency. He picked up after a few rings.

"Ayo Silk it's me. I'm in fucking Belize man. That nigga Fe set me up. I'm good right now though and I'm gonna see how this shit plays out. They're keeping me alive for a reason."

"What the fuck happened bruh." He asked sounding relieved and mad at the same damn time.

"I'll give you all the details when I get back. But I need you to do me a favor and get up with LaLa and let her know what's up. She didn't pick up her phone when I called."

"Look Messiah... Shorty ain't good right now. She's fucked up and in the hospital."

"The fuck you mean Silk?"

"She got hit bruh and it's touch and go right now. To keep shit real, it's not looking too good for her or the baby."

I felt myself losing control and slammed my fist into the table breaking that shit to pieces. There wasn't a single fucking thing I could do for my wife or my baby hundreds of miles away, being kept in a whole other fucking country. I didn't know when I was gonna make it back either.

"Make sure she stays good while I find a way to get back there nigga. Hold shit down and find out who the fuck did this shit to her."

"Already."

I ended the call with Silk right after that because talking about the shit he just told me was fuckin' me up more in the head right now. There wasn't shit I could do for Larissa right now with me being held down here in Belize and that had me about to go crazy. Then to hear him say she and my baby might not make it was too much. I needed to get the fuck back home and take care of my fucking family. I knew how shit went in the game and that at any moment those you loved could be taken from you. But LaLa wasn't about to fucking die on me. I couldn't imagine my life without her.

Larissa

I heard the sounds of a machine beeping and it was getting on my nerves so bad. I just wanted the noise to stop. I struggled to open my eyes to see where the hell the irritating sound was coming from. But when I opened my eyes, I realized I was in a damn hospital and my body instantly started hurting as I moved.

There was a shooting pain in my chest and I tried to touch where the pain was mainly coming from right between my breasts, but there was a big ass bandage covering the area.

That's when everything started coming back to me. From being shot when I opened the door at the hotel and even coming in and out of consciousness on the ambulance ride to the hospital. I moved my hand down to my stomach and sighed a breath of relief when I felt the baby bump was still there. The only difference was it felt so much bigger than I remembered. My stomach was big as hell and that didn't make sense because I was only a couple months pregnant and barely showing when I was shot.

I tried to scoot up to be in more of a sitting position and get more comfortable, but when I did I heard a voice that scared me to death and made me jump.

"Shorty I'm glad you're finally up. Let me get the nurse."

"Wait, Draco. Where's Messiah? How long have I been in here? How's my baby?"

"Damn LaLa I'm happy as fuck you're awake but you got to relax with the 21 questions shit. Let someone check your ass out and make sure you're good and then I'll answer some shit." Draco said with a serious ass face.

I probably overwhelmed him from my questions but I needed to know what the hell was going on. Draco was the wild one out of the group and not really the best one to answer my questions anyway. But he was the only one here. Which made me wonder why Messiah wasn't here. Shanice wasn't here either. Everything just seemed off about the whole situation and my intuition was telling me that something was wrong.

After the nurse and doctor both checked me out Shanice stormed into the hospital room damn near running. She was screaming and smiling ear to ear excited to see that I was really awake.

"Damn bitch took you long enough!" She said as she sat down on the edge of my bed and started crying.

"Shanice what the hell is going on girl? I woke up to Draco being here instead of my man and his ass avoided all my questions. How long have I been here and what's really up?"

"I'm just so glad you're finally awake and talking to me. Larissa you been in here for the past 3 months girl. You're almost six months pregnant and we been waiting for you to come up out of the coma you was in. You had me scared to death. The doctor's didn't think you was gonna pull through at first, but wasn't no way we were giving up on you."

"Shanice you mean to tell me I been in here three months? Why isn't Messiah here?"

She looked away and there was an awkward pause that let me know I was about to hear some shit I wasn't gonna like.

"He's in Belize girl. He calls to check on you every day but he's been there since the day your accident happened."

Tears started to fall from my eyes soaking my face and the front of my hospital gown. I moved my hands over my stomach and started rubbing my now very large baby bump. Everything she said was too much to take in. I had been in a traumatic situation and almost lost mine and my baby's life. Yet my man was nowhere to be found. He was off in Belize instead of by my side. There could have been a good reason why he was away and not here. But none of that shit mattered. The fact remained he knew I was laid up here in a fucking coma. He wasn't the person I woke up to when he should have been.

Messiah calling every day didn't make the situation any better either. If he could call it was obvious that he was choosing to be away from me and our baby growing inside me. The shit was breaking my heart again. I thought he was really it for me. That he was gonna be by my side even if we didn't work out. He promised to take care of me and not betray me and yet he did.

"Girl, don't cry. You and Jr. are fighters. Ya'll beat the odds and are here. You got your whole life ahead of you. Don't let that nigga get to you. He might have a good reason why he's not here."

"Neesy, he knew I was in here. He been calling and shit but can't come. Let me ask you this, how many times has he been up here to see me?"

I looked at her and all she could do was shake her head because she knew what I was saying was nothing but the truth. There wasn't any excuse for how he'd done me.

"I'm gonna be good though girl. I got my life and my baby, so I'm gonna just live now. Messiah can do the same and stay the fuck away from us."

Draco and Silk came into the room soon after. As soon as they came in I made sure to give them a message for their homeboy.

"Tell that nigga I don't want him calling and checking on me. Tell him not to worry about me anymore. And thanks for being here with me, but it's time ya'll stay the fuck away from me too. You two can leave." I said that shit with finality.

It was really time to live my life without Messiah being a part of it. I would always be grateful for the time we spent together and the love we shared. I wouldn't take any of it back and had been blessed with the life that was growing inside me. But I couldn't share a future with a man who wasn't there for me when I needed him most. I needed to look out for my best interests even if no one else did.

Messiah (Money)

I was lying in a big ass comfortable king size bed in the middle of fucking paradise and all my mind kept thinking about was Larissa. I had been in Belize for the last few months after Fe and Torio brought me down here on some snake ass shit. They went against the plug with the shit they pulled.

That nigga was head of the largest cartel in Belize. He was in charge of all the drugs shipped through Belize from Mexico and Columbia. Any product that moved to the US from Belize came by way of this nigga. He was not to be fucked with and was a heartless mothafucka.

It turned out the same nigga, my plug, running the whole damn country of Belize was my no good ass father. The same man I had never even met my whole fuckin' life and who had basically said fuck me was now trying to take me under his wing and have me as his right hand.

Emeri wanted me to take over his cartel one day. I wasn't with all that emotional shit and neither was he apparently. But blood meant something to him and he didn't trust any other mothafucka in the world to do the job when he was gone.

When Fe and Torio blew my car up and held my ass hostage my father Emeri came through and set some shit up where the two believed he was handing over his entire operation to them. But those two were some stupid mothafuckas to think they could outsmart him. He easily found where they were keeping me and brought me to his fifteen acre estate without a problem from either of them.

Now Fe and Torio were both on the run while my father had half the world looking for their asses. I would be looking for their ass's too after I played this shit out with my so called father.

I told my niggas back home to find the mothafuckas responsible for hitting up LaLa and there wasn't a single lead which let me know it must have been Fe and Torio who were responsible. They were gonna pay for it with their lives one way or another and I would make sure that I pulled the trigger when the time came.

I found out that Fe was actually my uncle and Torio was his son, making him my cousin. It was like I had a whole fucking family out here that I never knew anything about. I didn't know why my mother kept all this shit from me and when I got back to NC and saw her in person I was gonna ask.

My father gave me an option of returning to the US and going back to my regular life but the catch was he would no longer supply any of the drugs for my operation. The other choice he gave me was to stay in Belize for 6 months and learn the ropes to his organization so I would be prepared to take over when the time came. I didn't want to go back to looking for a new plug and basically being back at square one so I took him up on his offer.

The shit with Larissa and my baby was what was really fucking with me. I made a promise to myself to never put a bitch or anyone before making money. So that was another reason why I chose to stay in Belize even when I knew she was in the hospital in a fucking coma. On top of that I felt like the shit would have never happened to her in the first place if she wasn't involved with me. It was best if I just left her alone and let her live her life without the danger I was putting her in.

I was still gonna take care of my son. Deep down I knew LaLa was a fighter and her and my son would pull through. Even though I made the choice to leave her alone, I made sure to have Silk and Draco keep an eye on her. I called every day to check on her condition. I was always gonna make sure she was straight too and there wasn't a doubt in my mind that I would always love her. It was just better for both of us if we went our separate ways.

The bitch lying next to me was some dark skin freak I had been fucking with for the past few weeks. She was shaped similar to Larissa but nowhere near on her level. Her name was Che and to make it so bad her name meant "don't do it" in Garifuna.

My father and his family were part of the country's Garifuna people. They basically did the impossible with coming out of having nothing to being the ones who ran the damn country. Shit my father Emeri had the entire government on his payroll.

I was fuckin' around with some other bitches besides Che but her ass kept me company most nights since I met her. She could at least hold a conversation with me and didn't bother me with bullshit. So I tolerated her ass more than the other bitches.

No matter what though all of this was just something to do while I was here. I already knew I would never love another woman the way I loved Larissa. I would love that girl for the rest of my life. She was the total package and more than that she had earned my respect and trust which was more valuable than any other shit. My heart was cold to all these other females and wasn't nothing changing that.

"That's that shit I like shorty."

Somehow Che had made her way under the covers and had my dick in her hand while she circled the tip with her tongue. She continued Circling the head and let the spit drip down. She began jacking me off until my dick was a fucking brick and she deep throated my shit. I could feel her damn tonsils and then she started to move her head up and down fast as hell closing the back of her throat each time she moved up.

She must have felt me tense up and she tried to hop on my dick real quick. I wasn't about to let that shit happen though. I didn't want any other girl out here to carry my seeds besides LaLa so I pushed her back and sat up in bed. I reached into my bedside table drawer and pulled out a condom before putting it on my dick. Then I laid back and let Che climb on top of me while my legs were still hanging over the side of the bed.

She positioned herself where she was straddling me and began sucking on my neck. I lifted her up and let my dick stretch her pussy wide as she came down. I lay there and moved my hands up to play with her titties while she rode my dick. She could catch my nut but I wasn't really into fucking her this morning. LaLa was heavy on my mind and I couldn't seem to stop thinking about her.

While Che bounced up and down on my dick I closed my eyes and pictured it was LaLa I was fucking instead. I grabbed ahold of her hips and started bringing her up and down hard as hell making a slapping noise each time I was all the way in. Her juices were gushing out and I wanted her to go even harder like LaLa did when she was riding my dick so I pushed her torso back so that she was arched back more with my hand on her chest between her titties.

With my other hand I found her clit and moved my fingers back and forth hard on it. That shit had Che going even harder so I grabbed her ass rough as hell squeezing the fuck out of it making her pussy feel tighter and I let my nut fill the condom up.

I opened my eyes back up just to be fucked up in the head all over again by the fact that Larissa wasn't the one looking back down at me. That shit was the best fuck I've had since being in Belize and away from my girl. The fucked up part was I had imagined it was her I was fucking instead of Che who was the one actually riding my dick.

"Hinsietibu áliegua baba" (*I love fucking you daddy!*)

I guess my big ass dick had Che caught up in her feelings since she let her native language of Garifuna come out. I didn't understand shit she said when she used it but it was probably better that way. I tapped her thigh to let her know I was ready for her to get up so I could get the condom off my dick. I went into the huge ass bathroom I had connected to my master suite.

Emeri who was my father in name alone pretty much, had me staying at his estate. The shit was so damn big that it had three completely separate wings. Basically each section was their own fucking house by themselves. I didn't need all this room since it was just me and the bitches who I entertained from time to time. My real family was back

25

home and would be kept far away from anything that could put them in danger, like me.

After washing and getting dressed for the day I went down to see what my father had planned for the day. He wanted me out here for business so that was my only concern at the end of the day. I needed to make sure the money kept flowing into Money Makers Inc. back home and would try and stack more in the process.

So far, I had met the bosses of the Mexican and Columbian cartels that relied on my father's transport routes to get their shit to the states at a good rate and with little problems from customs. It was time I get to know the ins and outs of how my father's accounts worked and how his team fully functioned.

I was making rounds with my father when I received a coded text from Draco. The text he sent let me know it was something to do with Larissa and it was important. I sat in the passenger seat of the Maserati we were riding in for the day and took out a blunt I already had rolled to smoke. Since being in Belize I had started smoking more than I ever had. Not as much as Draco's ass, but more than usual. It helped to keep me calm and stay focused when it seemed like I was out of my fucking element, which was all the time down here.

As soon as we finished for the day I rushed out of the car and over to my section of the property. I wanted to have complete privacy when I called Draco back or anyone for that matter. I didn't trust these mothafuckas one bit. It didn't matter that Emeri was my biological father or his team would someday work for me, he hadn't been in my life since I was born. I never forgot shit a mothafucka did to me. I didn't give a fuck about the nigga one way or the other and just wanted to make as much money off of him as I could.

I dialed my boy's number and waited for his ass to pick up which seemed like forever considering his text had me worried something was wrong with LaLa's condition.

"Bruh, what's up?" I asked as soon as he said hello.

"LaLa woke up man. I'm not even gonna lie nigga, she flipped the fuck out as soon as she realized you was MIA."

"Word. She'll get over that shit. I gotta do what's best for her and that means leaving her ass alone. She and the baby are good though right?"

"Yeah they're good Money. When the fuck you coming back? Shit's not right without you man."

"I got a few more months and then I'll be back like I never fuckin' left. Hold shit down and make sure you have eyes on my family at all times."

"Alright nigga, One."

27

I hung up the phone and went back inside leaving the patio where I made the call from. The shit with Larissa had me relieved and mad as hell at the same time. I threw my phone against the living room wall and it broke instantly. I snatched the table beside the couch and flung that shit against the wall too. Then I started punching the fucking wall back to back leaving two big ass holes, causing my knuckles to bleed. By the time I was done breaking shit and making a fucking mess I still wasn't feeling better.

I didn't really have a reason to be mad since I was the one who made the decision to leave Larissa alone. It was more me being mad at my damn self. I made promises to her. I made her trust me and here I was doing all the shit I said I wouldn't do. I was a hood nigga who lived by my word. But this shit had me being exactly the type of nigga I never wanted to be.

Larissa was more than my heart. She was my fucking everything and I knew I fucked her over in the worst way. I knew she was going to be fucking broken behind my actions. I understood LaLa inside and out and if she was hurting then I was hurting too, but this time I wasn't gonna do anything about it. I had to find a way to let her go no matter how hard it was because in the long run it would be better for both of us.

Larissa

Life returned to somewhat normal for me over the last few month except for a few things. I moved out of the place Messiah and me were sharing as soon as I was released from the hospital. He fucked me over for the second time in the short amount of time we were together. There wasn't a doubt in my mind that I loved him but I would not be a weak woman who didn't value myself. So I made the decision to move on.

I was doing pretty well with moving on because the reality of the shooting really got to me. Here I was eighteen, just graduated high school, pregnant, and recovering from a gunshot wound to the chest. I almost lost my life behind Messiah. Even though he didn't pull the trigger, he promised to protect me from the dangers that came with his life. But he failed to keep even his ex from touching me. I knew exactly who shot me even though every time Shanice asked I told her I didn't get a good look at who it was.

When I answered the door thinking it was room service Messiah's damn baby mama was standing there instead. As soon as I had the door all the way open it was already too late to see the gun she was aiming at me. Then came the burning in my chest. The pain was the worst I had ever felt and all I could think about was my baby and Messiah's ass as I lost consciousness.

So to be alive was a blessing in itself. Then to come out of it okay and with my unborn child not only survive but to be unaffected was more than I could hope for. So even though I was hurt by Messiah's actions I wasn't letting him consume my time or energy. I truly felt like a new person and was grateful for every single day I was alive.

My due date was next week but I had been having contractions all morning so I called up Shanice to come pick me up so I could get checked out. The pain so far was only a tightening feeling so I wasn't really sure if I was in labor but I wasn't about to take any chances. She came running in the house and grabbed my bag fast as hell before basically pushing me out the front door to make me move faster. She was so funny I couldn't do nothing but laugh at her.

We arrived at the hospital a few minutes later since my apartment was near downtown which was close by. My contractions started getting stronger and I was in a lot more pain. Once I was seen by the nurse I was told that I was four centimeters and was in labor. I got more nervous and scared. I didn't know if I was really ready to be a mother but there wasn't no turning back now. Shanice was by my side throughout the entire delivery and after hours and hours of pain it was all worth it.

I welcomed Messiah Jamir Lawson Jr into the world. I named him after Messiah despite how he had done me because regardless of everything I knew he would be a good father. I wasn't gonna get in the way of that.

"Girl he looks just like Money's ass I swear!"

Shanice said exactly what I was thinking as I looked over at my perfect baby in the hospital crib he was in.

"Don't I know it." I replied while admiring the creation me and Messiah made.

I didn't understand why Messiah stayed away in Belize but it would have been nice for him to make an attempt to see MJ's birth. I figured by now one of his boys would have filled him in on the birth of his son. Shanice and Silk were still going strong and were living together and everything. She wasn't into running her mouth so I wasn't worried about things getting back to Messiah for the most part, but I was pretty sure she told Silk where she was.

I spent two days in the hospital and then MJ and me both were released. Shanice came and picked us up from the hospital and took us to my place. Being a new mom was a big change. I was exhausted and learning how to be a mother was a struggle. There was nothing I wouldn't do for my son though. He came into my life and made everything worthwhile. Every day he grew and learned so much. Easter was coming and I was excited that he would get to celebrate his first holiday already at almost 2 months old.

Messiah was having money deposited into my bank account weekly. The amounts were crazy as hell too. There was no way I was gonna spend all the money. I bought a car the week after I had MJ because having a newborn I needed to be able to get around without having to depend on other people for rides. I bought a white Lexus SUV that I fell in love with the minute I saw it. But otherwise, I really wasn't trying to spend his money unless it was something for MJ.

Today I planned on taking MJ to the mall to see the Easter Bunny and take pictures. He was seven weeks old so I finally felt more comfortable taking him in public. Shanice was going to meet me there with a couple of her baby cousins she was bringing too.

After having MJ my body had not gotten right back in shape but I still looked good. There was more meat on my thighs and ass but it fit my body. My stomach wasn't exactly flat either but with the clothes I wore no one could tell. I was still self-conscious about how I looked since having the baby but Shanice reassured me constantly that I was still killing the bitches.

I wore a pink button up shirt with some white jeans and some ones. My hair had grown so much while I was recovering in the hospital that it was now shoulder length. I let the red highlights grow out and added some blond ones to make it work. MJ was wearing white pants and a blue shirt to coordinate with me.

We arrived later than I told Shanice we would be. I was still getting used to going places with a newborn and it took so much longer for every little thing it seemed like. I wrapped MJ in a blanket and carried him in my arms while I walked with his baby bag over my shoulder. I hurried up and made my way over to the Easter section where the pictures were.

Shanice was waiting for me with a couple of cute little kids that looked nothing like her. They were probably around four or five and there was a boy and a girl who were each dressed up matching each other. We stood in line and waited until it was time to take our pictures. Shanice went ahead and positioned her cousins where she thought they looked best before letting the picture be taken.

Then I went ahead and stood next to the dressed up easter bunny holding MJ at an angle where he could be seen. Just as we got settled and I was smiling I saw Messiah's ass walk up like he owned the damn place. Of course he came and stood next to me with his arm around me and a smile on his face.

My body tensed up and I cringed. I kept a smile on my face and didn't say a single word to his ass though. He was really trying me right now. To disappear and leave me and then to wait until this moment to meet his son. Messiah truly had some fucked up ways and I wasn't about to try and make sense of them. I needed to remember that all of our interactions at this point were for MJ only and so the other bullshit was irrelevant anyway.

After we took pictures I walked away without trying to spark up a conversation. I really didn't have shit to say to his ass anyway.

"Larissa slow down shorty. Let me holla at you real quick."

"What Messiah?" I turned around and said while rolling my eyes.

I wasn't trying to cause a scene so I kept my voice down. I didn't think the mall was the time or the place for this conversation to take place. But I knew Messiah well enough to know that if he wanted something he got it no matter who was around or what anyone else wanted.

"Chill ma. I know I got some explaining. But right now I just wanted to meet my son."

"Alright." I said calmly and gently placed MJ in his father's arms.

Messiah started smiling like a goofy little kid. He looked like the happiest man alive. I couldn't even lie, Messiah holding MJ made me feel happy too. I was glad that my son got to finally meet his father. MJ deserved to have his father in his life, even if I didn't want him in mine. Messiah handed MJ back to me and then tried to continue the conversation.

"LaLa I'm sorry for how shit went down. Just know that I love ya'll no matter what. I'm gonna always take care of my son. This right here is my fucking heart." He said while pointing to me and MJ. "Even though we not together I'm gonna be a father to him and be in his life. Right now I gotta be in Belize for a while longer but when I get back permanently we'll set some shit up for me keeping him some."

He caught me off guard with the last part but I played it off. I wasn't trying to be in his business and worry about what was going on with Messiah's ass anymore. So I shrugged and nodded my head.

"Cool. Well I better be going. Get up with me when you're back and we'll figure it out. Bye Messiah."

I turned and walked away with my head held high even if my heart was heavy. I would never let him see me hurt over how dirty he had done me. I felt that us going our separate ways really was for the best. He still gave me those butterflies when I was near him but the betrayal was too much. Maybe one day another man would have the same effect on me. One thing was for sure, and that was me and Messiah were officially over.

Messiah (Money)

I pulled up Larissa's location as soon as I touched down in the states last night. I was here on business but wanted to see my son in person for the first time and LaLa too. I didn't want to be alone with her ass yet though because I didn't trust myself enough to be around her and not try and fuck yet. Shit even seeing her at the mall had my dick hard as hell. I even missed smelling that damn perfume she always wore. I had to control myself because even at the mall I was liable to fuck her so I'm glad she was holding MJ.

She was still bad as fuck too even after giving birth to our son. Her ass was fatter and titties bigger but otherwise she really hadn't changed much. The fact that she gave me my first son made me love her ass more if that was possible.

I would have liked to spend more time with my lil man, but right now I wasn't really here on the family tip. It was already past the original six months I agreed to stay in Belize, but I added a few months to the deal. I needed to really gain Emeri's full trust before I felt comfortable taking any of my attention off of the business at hand.

Not only for personal gain and building my enterprise but because Emeri had a long reach. Going against him even a little could put my family in danger. So for the time being it was best if I just kept focused on making him believe I was trustworthy and when the time was right I would make moves to ensure my family's safety and get shit settled in Belize.

I needed to discuss some shit with Silk and Draco so I headed over to Draco's place first to pick his ass up. I called him before stopping by but his phone went straight to voicemail. I didn't have time to wait for his slow ass so I decided to pick him up on the way to pick up Silk. I didn't even have enough time to wait on meeting up at the warehouse since Emeri wanted me to fly back tonight. I was far from a fuckin' do boy, so this shit was for the damn birds. I was gonna be patient though and play my cards right.

I knocked on the door to Draco's townhouse which was in the same building I put Carina up in. I didn't have time to stop by and see my baby girl this time but I would when I came back in town for good. I wanted to avoid Carina's stupid ass too because she would be trying to fuck and whether me or Larissa was together or not I wasn't trying to go back down that road again.

Draco came to the door and let me into his house. We walked over to the dining room and he pulled out a blunt before sitting down on the bar stool to put his shoes on. I stood there in a daze because this nigga let me in his house and acted like nothing was going on. Right in the damn living room a few feet away two fine ass bitches was going at it.

One of them was sitting on the couch completely naked playing with her titties while another bitch was on the floor in front of her eating her pussy. The chick on the floor still hadn't even looked up to see who I was. She was gripping the other bitch's thighs and squatted down with her ass sitting up nice as fuck.

The girl on the couch was looking back and forth between Draco and me smiling. She had some sexy dimples that were pierced and long ass hair that made it look like she had some Indian in her or some shit.

Draco lit the blunt and called out to the two causing them to stop for the minute.

"Yo Keisha ya'll got to go. I'm 'bout to bounce."

"But Draco we was just getting started. Plus we wanted some more dick and your friend just got here." She said with a pout on her face.

Draco looked at me and shrugged his shoulders to let me know he was cool with the shit so I walked over to the two women. Both of them stood up and looked me up and down. I told them to turn around and they did without a word. I slapped each of them on the ass and watched as that shit shook from the impact. They were both sexy but I would have to pass on fuckin' with them this time. I didn't have time to get sidetracked by bitches and no pussy came before business ever.

I wasn't in a relationship anymore so I went back to being the heartless young nigga I was before LaLa. There wasn't no woman alive who could make me feel like she could or who's pussy felt like it was meant for me besides Larissa. Draco lit the blunt and we left the house as soon as the girls got their shit together and bounced.

I drove over to Silk's house with Draco's ass in the backseat like usual. Silk wasn't even riding yet but he still sat back there. Once Silk got in it was time to fill both my niggas in on all the shit that was going on.

"I'm staying in Belize for two more months learning how my pops operation run then I'll be back like I never fuckin' left. The mothafucka thinks he won me over and I'm down for whatever he says. I'm playing shit cool right now but after I touch back down for good we gotta start planning to get rid of his ass. Ain't no way I'm gonna be a bitch out here taking orders and shit. We can take control of the whole cartel once he's gone. That's why I'm out there for now making him think I'm on his team."

"Damn bruh, cartels are serious fucking business. You sure you want do this shit?" Draco asked with a serious look on his face.

He was usually down for whatever so his hesitation had me wondering what the fuck his problem was.

"You scared or some shit nigga? You know I don't work for no other mothafucka alive and I'm not about to start now. The fact that my so called father is teaching me how to run the cartel makes the shit that much easier. That man didn't raise me and blood don't make a nigga family. At the end of the day I'm trying to get this mothafuckin' money and be the boss of it all. So what the fuck's the problem?

"Damn Money chill the fuck out. That nigga's still your father, and this shit gonna cause a lot of fall out. I'm one hundred nigga and gonna ride regardless. I hope you know what you're doing nigga. You got a whole family out here you basically pushing to the side for this shit so it better be worth it."

"What the fuck you say? Nigga don't speak on shit you don't know. Larissa and my son are good. Don't ever bring some shit up to me that don't concern you again. This got nothing to do with them. This is business and I thought your ass knew the fuckin' difference."

"Ya'll chill out bruh. What you're telling us is a big fucking deal Money. Draco is just speaking facts nigga. We're with you no matter what so you ain't got to worry. As soon as you get back we'll figure out the best way to make the shit happen. We'll hold shit down here in the meantime." Silk spoke up.

He knew me and Draco would go toe to toe whenever we disagreed. We were both hot headed and passionate about the shit we spoke on. We were first cousins but more like

41

brothers so we were too much alike at times. Silk was the calm and composed one who had a level head and kept us from going at it plenty of times.

The shit Draco said still had me feeling some type of way since he brought up my family. He should know better than question me about them. The business shit he was talking about was understandable but my personal life was off limits unless I asked for his damn opinion. If he didn't agree with how I was handling shit it wasn't his fucking place to say.

I had one more place to go before catching my flight. I pulled up to my mother's house and got out. This was the meeting that Emeri sent me here for. He had a message he wanted me to give my mother in person. I was holding a letter addressed to her from Emeri. I didn't open it or read it because whatever they had going on didn't have shit to do with me.

"Ma, I'm home."

I called out as I used my key to open the front door. My mother came out from the back. She was wearing some jeans and a tank top. She was a beautiful woman and looked way younger than she was. My mom could pass for being in her thirties rather than her fifties which she was. She came over to me and gave me a hug. It was good to see her after such a long ass time of being away. She went over to the kitchen and sat at the table.

"Where you been Messiah? I appreciate you having your friends let me know you were okay. But son, I haven't seen or heard from you in months. You had me worried to death. What's going on?" She asked me straight out like I figured she would.

My mother always spoke her mind and hated to hold anything back. Instead of replying I walked into the kitchen and placed the letter I brought on the table in front of her. She eyed me strangely and so I nodded my head to indicate she should just read the letter. She tore it from the envelope and then slowly read the letter and then read it over again before her eyes met mine. She had tears in her eyes. Whatever was in the letter affected her.

"I'm sorry son. Let me explain." I held my hand up and shook my head no.

"It's all good. I'll be back in a few months for good and you can tell me everything then. We're straight."

She stood up and we hugged. I left out of the house and felt a weight lifted off of me as well. Even if I didn't know the reason why she lied about my father I knew it had come from a good place. My mother was always there for me and raised me and my brothers on her own. So I couldn't fault her if she kept some shit from me.

It was time for me to head back to Belize. Being back home made me even more ready to get this shit over with and come back. It was bittersweet seeing everyone knowing I wasn't gonna see them again for a few more months. The life I lived, tomorrow wasn't promised so that made the shit even harder. I missed my niggas and my hood and I needed to be here for my kids.

Most of all I missed LaLa and the life we had been building together. I loved that girl still which was the only good thing about going back to Belize. She was better off without me in her life bringing her pain and disappointment. So maybe staying away longer would make it easier for both of us to move on.

Silk

Me and Shanice had been going strong for the past five months and the more time we spent together the more sure I was about her being the woman for me. I moved her ass in with me after the first semester of college was over. She ended up going to school right here in Wilmington so she could stay closer to Larissa after the shooting. You could tell a lot about a person by how they dealt with shit that came their way. The fact that she stayed by Larissa's side and never wavered showed me that she was a rider and the type of woman I could depend on.

Everything was going good between us and she wanted me to meet her family. I was fine with meeting them. But as the dinner she planned got closer Shanice started acting stressed the fuck out. I was just about ready to tell her to cancel the shit since it was making her act crazy as hell but decided to let her be because I loved her ass.

I was me and no mothafucka alive was gonna make me feel less than. She told me all about how her family was uppity and thought they were too good for people from the hood. I would be respectful to them because they were Shanice's parents but I was a thug from the hood so I already knew they weren't gonna want their daughter to have shit to do with me. If meeting her parents was something that was important to Shanice then I would put up with it without a complaint.

I spent even more time in the streets over the past couple months with Money gone. Running our operation was left up to me and Draco so we had to pull the extra weight Money usually did. That meant more nights out, more time enforcing shit and more time in the office too. We owned several successful businesses that were legal to run along with the drug shit.

So far me and Draco kept shit running smoothly without any major problems. Money was coming back in a few weeks. As soon as he touched back down we were gonna expand to the surrounding states. We needed to finalize our plans and go over everything in person. I didn't doubt my nigga for a second. He was built for this life and his mind stayed working twenty four hours a day.

I disagreed with how Money pushed his family to the side to focus on our business shit. But it wasn't my place to question him. If he came to me for some advice I'd be happy to give my opinions but otherwise I wasn't the type of nigga to get involved in my homies personal shit. It was his life and he could do whatever the fuck he wanted.

Draco felt like if Money could turn his back on his woman and seed then there wasn't shit stopping him from turning his back on us. I didn't agree with his ass either, but he was a grown ass man who could think what he wanted too. The two of them had the same damn temper and always spoke their mind without giving a fuck who liked what they said. You could definitely tell they were related. I hoped shit calmed down between them once Money got back because I was tired of playing peace maker between the two.

Shanice came downstairs with a church dress on. She convinced me to go to church with her and then have Sunday dinner at her parent's house afterwards. I was dressed in a black polo suit with some Giuseppe shoes. Shanice had her natural hair out and I loved that shit.

"I'm ready. We can go." She said that shit with a little attitude showing me she was still on edge about having me meet her parents.

Instead of saying anything back I nodded my head and followed behind her. Even though she was dressed modest in the church dress her ass still looked sexy as fuck. With each step she took her ass switched back and forth. As I watched her walk the shit made me want to take her back upstairs and fuck before we left. We didn't have time for that if we were gonna make the church service though so I let her keep walking this time.

The service was awkward as hell for me. I had been to church plenty of times coming up. My grandma always took me with her so it wasn't like I was ignorant to the shit. What made it so weird was the way the service went and how all the people acted. It wasn't the same type of uplifting service I was used to.

Everybody sat still and quiet basically the whole time. The service only lasted an hour too which was surprising as hell because every service I ever went to lasted at least three hours. There was mostly white folks and that alone had me feeling out of place. I wasn't expecting none of this shit when Shanice asked me to go to church with her. After the service we met up with her parents in the hallway.

"Shanice it's so nice to see you dear." Her mother said while pulling her in for a hug and kissing her on the cheek. Shanice hugged her back.

"I missed you too mom. Mom, Dad this is my boyfriend Kenneth." She looked at her mom and dad as she said the last part.

Both of them stared at me and then back at Shanice. The look of disapproval was written all over their faces but I decided to keep my mouth shut because they were Shanice's parents. If any other mothafucka looked at me wrong I would fuck them up without question. I was a street nigga not one of those little weak ass niggas they wanted their daughter to end up with. Her parents were just going to have to get that shit out of their head because there was no way I was letting Shanice go. She was my baby and not even her parents were gonna come between us that was for damn sure.

"Really Shanice?" Her father questioned in a stern voice.

He was really trying some shit right here while we were in the church. He wasn't even waiting for the dinner at their house to start the bullshit. I was waiting for Shanice to respond. She locked her fingers in mine and began to walk away while keeping my hand in hers. She managed to mumble a goodbye and never turned back.

"I'm sorry Silk. I should have known better. My parents act like they're better than everybody else even though they came from the same damn hood. It's always some bullshit. I just wanted them to at least give you a chance." Shanice said to me once we made it back in the car.

She had tears in her eyes which was out of character for her since she always tried to play tough like she didn't give a fuck. Shanice loved and respected her parents and only wanted their approval. She had different views about people than them and they obviously couldn't get past that shit for the benefit of their own fucking daughter. Seeing her this upset made me wanna go back in the church and lay them both down that's how much I cared about her. But I would never hurt her like that by harming her parents.

"It's cool baby. Don't sweat it. I'm not going nowhere. They'll get their shit together and get over the choices you make. They love you shorty and just want what's best for you."

49

"Thanks bae. I needed to hear that. But you're what's best for me." She leaned in and began kissing me deep and slow showing me how much she appreciated what I told her.

My dick was ready to be inside her already so I put the car in gear and headed home so we could make that shit happen.

Larissa

It seemed like time was flying by. MJ was already four months old and getting bigger by the day. I was finally at peace completely with how things had turned out for me. Not that my life was over or anything. I was still young and had a full life ahead of me to look forward to hopefully. I spent enough time crying and getting over Messiah while I was being a stay at home mom the past couple of months. I finally felt comfortable about where I was at.

My main focus now was being the best mother I could to MJ and accomplishing my goals for college and then having a successful career. I was starting to feel like my life was getting on the right track. I no longer cried myself to sleep every night over Messiah and I thought about him less and less as time went on. I still thought about what we could have been especially when I looked at my son because he looked so much like his father. But the pain I felt became bearable.

I registered for summer session at the college. I was gonna attend classes on campus and work on completing my bachelor's degree in graphic design. I wanted to become a web-designer and open my own business. So I was also going to minor in business to learn all the basic shit I would need.

Shanice called me earlier to try and get me to go out with her to the club. She said Silk was going out of town on business and she needed to get out to celebrate midterms being over and Spring Break next week. She really had been stressing her midterms this semester and said messing with Silk was a distraction. Knowing my girl she still pulled As and Bs in all her classes. She was naturally smart and made a big deal out of nothing when it came to school.

She talked me into going out and I planned on leaving MJ with Ms. Sheila. She really stepped up and was the absolute best grandmother to my son that I could have hoped for. She watched him at least once a week and let me know she would gladly watch him while I was at school in the future. That alone lifted a big burden off of me not having to worry about putting him in daycare at such a young age.

Ms. Sheila never brought up Messiah and we actually had a pretty good relationship. I looked up to her as a mother figure and she always gave me good advice about my future and school. She even tried to get me to open up to the idea of dating again down the road.

I was still somewhat uncomfortable with my body since having the baby. I wasn't all the way back down to the size I was before MJ. I used to be a size seven and now was more of a nine or eleven. I was insecure of my stomach which seemed like the worst part on my body especially after the toned flat waist I used to have. I didn't know what I was gonna wear out for the night.

I wanted to feel sexy for the first time since before being pregnant, which seemed like forever ago. I finally chose a red bodysuit with a deep v cut neckline and a high waisted black skirt that had a slit to my thigh. I picked out some shoes to match and went ahead and got in the shower. After I got out I packed up the outfit and the rest of my things for the night and headed over to Shanice's. We were gonna get ready at her and Silk's place tonight.

I was happy for my best friend. She found a man who matched her perfectly. The two of them were funny as hell to me. They stayed cracking jokes and arguing, but both of them had a soft spot for each other. The dysfunctional shit worked for their crazy asses somehow. As soon as I arrived over at their place I went up to the door and knocked on it. I didn't bother calling first because she told me to come right over after dropping MJ off with Ms. Sheila. After the second knock Silk opened the door.

"Shit. I didn't know you was coming over." He said to me almost as an apology.

I didn't know his ass was gonna be here either I thought. I was somewhat taken back by his tone because I showed up here all the time and it never was a problem. He rubbed his fresh fade with his hand like he was stressed about something before he opened the door wider to let me in.

"Nice to see you too Silk." I said sarcastically.

He shrugged and then walked further into the house and made his way into the living room. Their place had beige carpet and white furniture. There was a big ass fireplace in the corner of the room and there wasn't any decor anywhere except a gigantic picture of Shanice and Silk hanging over the mantel. They were staring in each other's eyes while Silk had his arms wrapped around Shanice with his hands grabbing her ass. The picture wasn't just his with his hands resting on her ass either, but actually squeezing the shit. I thought the picture was a perfect representation of their love and relationship.

Shanice was laid out on the couch, wrapped in a blanket with her tablet in her hand. I knew her ass was in here reading. Her ass was always reading but I couldn't say anything because I did the same thing when I was home. I sat the outfit and bag I brought down in the empty chair. Shanice was still so into her book she hadn't even looked up at my ass. So I pushed her feet off the couch and sat down in their place. It was only ten o'clock so we had plenty of time to get ready and hyped up for the club before we left.

"Bitch you better get your ass up. You got me over here now so put that damn book down."

"Shit I just got into it good too. But you're right honey we got to get right for your first night back! All the niggas gonna be checking for you tonight."

"Whatever girl. I don't know if I'm ready for all that but you never know. I just wanna have a good time. We haven't been out together in forever."

"Yaaaas." Shanice shouted being all extra and loud.

That was my friend. I heard Silk go to the door again and open it. Footsteps came down the hall and I looked up to see who it was. Of course Messiah had to be the one standing there staring down at me with a look of lust on his face while I looked back at him.

That was just my damn luck and right before I was going out for the first time. I really wasn't checking for his ass anymore but the fact remained we had history together even if it was short lived and a son together. So I would be cordial with him but that was about it.

"Hey Messiah, what's up?"

"Just got back in town. I was gonna hit you up and see 'bout MJ."

"He's with your mama for the night if you wanna see him. Otherwise just get up with me tomorrow and we can set up an arrangement for his schedule."

"Where you going that he's staying overnight?"

This nigga really just asked me like it was his business what I did. He was not about to be in my business whatsoever.

55

"None of your business Messiah. Let's just keep shit cool between us and focus on raising our son. All that personal shit complicates things. I'm glad you're back but we really have nothing else to discuss."

"You got that shit." He copped an attitude real quick when he said the last part.

I didn't understand how he expected me to let him come back and try and check me. I wasn't about to fall victim to his charm or any of that shit that had worked in the past. He walked out of the room when Silk came back ready to head out. I knew his ass was mad, but he had no right to be.

We didn't exchange any more words and after he left I felt like I could breathe again. He still had my heart beating fast and caused butterflies in my stomach. He probably would always affect me that way, but I was proud of myself for handling the situation the way I did. I could have easily let him talk me into some shit from how he was looking at me. The last thing I needed to do was fuck around and complicate things more. Even if I was horny being around his ass.

Shanice and I went upstairs and began getting ready for our night out. She was wearing a skin tight gold dress that clung to her every curve. Her body was crazy and it was all natural unlike all those women who paid for theirs and ended up looking fake as hell. I kept my hair down and did a simple side part. Shanice slayed my face and I did hers before we finally were ready to leave for the club.

Me and Shanice threw back a couple shots of Henny while getting ready and I definitely was already feeling the effects of it. I hadn't had a drink since before the baby which was well over a year for me. I never was into drinking or partying heavy to begin with. I was gonna take it easy when we got to the club. The last thing I wanted to do was end up too fucked up.

We were going a little out of town on the Northside to a spot Shanice heard about from her cousin. I didn't know anything about the club scene so I didn't know what to expect from the place. Shanice didn't know much either but her cousin was already there tonight with some of her people so it put me at ease some. I just wanted to have a good time and not have to worry about some shit popping off.

Hopefully up here no one would know I was Money's ex and I wouldn't have to worry about his groupie bitches or niggas who wouldn't even look my way. I didn't know if I was anywhere near ready to date or take another man serious. It wasn't my focus right now that was for sure. But I wasn't completely out of the game either and could have fun if the opportunity presented itself.

We walked up to the front of the club and saw a line that was about twenty people deep. I had only been out a few times but never had to stand in line. Luckily before we even made it to the line the bouncers at the door spotted us walking up and gave us a head nod then waved us over. They were eye fucking us as we walked over too. We smiled at both their asses sweetly though.

"Ladies, ya'll good."

One of the doorman said while licking his lips and letting his eyes roam all over my body from head to toe. I smiled and blushed a little. I wasn't comfortable receiving compliments even though I was confident I never knew how to accept a person's admiration.

"Thanks." I replied.

He proceeded to put wristbands on our arms and stamp our hands. The other nigga lifted the red rope and let us walk in. I knew them two were still watching our asses while we walked past but that was all they would be getting from us. I didn't like thirsty niggas at all. I never was attracted to a man that had to chase pussy. Just like I would never chase after dick. It was important how a person carried themselves.

As soon as we walked in the club the vibe was immediately good. There was a lot of people but the building was bigger than the clubs downtown. Which was better than being all shoulder to shoulder with everybody. There was a big ass dancefloor and a stage on the side where a DJ was posted.

The place was nicer than I expected for its location. There was a few different bars located around the main room. They were playing good ass music already that had me two stepping while we made our way over to the bar closest to the dance floor.

Walking in we drew attention from every nigga without trying. One tried to slap my ass and when I turned around to talk shit a sexy ass man pushed him back before I even got an opportunity to put him in his place. I went to thank the man but he turned around and walked away without giving me a second look.

He was fine as hell and had a boss demeanor which made me wonder more about who he was. He had short hair and wore a hat. It was clear that he was a thug but he also seemed to be more than the typical nigga looking for attention. He carried himself like he was that nigga. It was too dark to get a really good look at his face but I had a feeling it was just as sexy as I pictured in my mind. I wasn't here to fall in love or no shit though so instead of wasting my time worrying about some passing nigga who checked a disrespectful man I shifted my attention back to following Shanice over to the bar.

Once I made it to the bar Shanice handed me the drink she already ordered since I had been stopped by the dumb shit on the way over. I began sipping it slowly and started trying to dance right by the damn bar. Shit I was here to have fun and turn up with my bitch. It was a night to celebrate so that was exactly what I was gonna do. Tomorrow I would get back focused on school and everything else I was trying to do.

Before heading out to the dance floor I checked my phone and saw a video clip Ms. Sheila sent me of MJ smiling and talking baby talk. I texted her real quick to check on him and she immediately messaged me back letting me know he was fine and she would call me in the morning. I was surprised her ass was up at this time of night anyway. After putting my phone back in my clutch I grabbed Shanice's hand and led her to the dance floor.

We got to the edge and slowly made our way somehow into the center of that shit. We were having a good time and really letting loose. It felt amazing to get out and just dance. We weren't going all out like some of the ratchet hoes out on the dance floor. We were definitely sexy and didn't need to be all extra. Our purpose wasn't to get niggas attention it was to enjoy ourselves.

After a few songs I got a strong feeling of someone watching me. A slow song came on and Shanice and me decided to take a break because we were out of breath and starting to sweat. We walked hand in hand to a side table by the bar and two niggas jumped up quick as hell to offer us a seat. Their bitches came and scooped them up right after so we didn't have to worry about them trying to holla either.

As we were talking I had the feeling of someone watching me again so I looked around and spotted the same nigga from earlier staring at me. He wasn't looking at me in a creepy way or anything. Once our eyes met, He raised his glass to me and I did the same in return with a huge ass smile plastered on my face. A few minutes later the bottle girl came over and tried to offer us some drinks supposedly from that same nigga. I wasn't a dumb girl about to get drugged in a club though so I politely turned down the drinks brought for us. I told the girl to let him know we weren't gonna accept a drink we didn't see fixed, but thanks anyway.

Shanice and I went ahead and ordered bottled waters because we didn't want to drink any more before we had to leave and drive back home. Especially because we were already feeling right.

While we were drinking our waters, the man from earlier decided to make an appearance. He stood right in front of me and our eyes stayed locked for a good minute. He clasped his hands together in front of himself near his crotch and I couldn't help but let my eyes wander down towards his dick. I quickly lifted my eyes back to his face but knew my ass was caught.

He was absolutely perfect in looks. He had a smooth dark brown complexion and a strong jaw. His eyes were sexy too and were drawing me in. He was a thug ass nigga and looking at him alone had my panties wet. I wasn't a hoe though so there wasn't any way he would have a chance of fucking me or anything. But there was nothing wrong with looking.

"I appreciate your caution but a nigga like me don't take no for an answer. I don't offer none of these hoes a mothafucking thing shorty, but you're different. I could tell from the moment I saw you walk in here."

He was still looking deep into my eyes and he seemed sincere with what he was saying. His attitude reminded me somewhat of Messiah, but I pushed that thought to the back of my mind as soon as I thought it.

"What you expect from me then?" I asked serious as hell.

He came all the way over here to tell me he wasn't gonna take no for an answer but his ass really hadn't even offered or asked me anything more than a drink. So I didn't know what his point was. Instead of saying anything back he grabbed a chair from another table and pulled it right next to me before sitting down.

He was close enough that our bodies were almost in contact with each other. I turned my head and gave him a questioning look and he just started bobbing his head to the music playing while he continued drinking from his cup. Then he placed his arm around my shoulders and I didn't object. When he did that shit my body actually responded right away and my heart rate sped up. It felt good to have him doing all this for me when he didn't even know my name yet.

"What are you doing?" I questioned again and this time he actually said something back.

"Shhhh, you fuckin' up our vibe right now. I'm trying to have a good time with your fine ass. You smell good as fuck and this shit feels right. You're the sexiest woman I've ever seen and I'm gonna make you mine."

"Oh yeah?"

"Damn right!"

"What's your name anyway?"

"Antoine."

We sat there for a few more minutes and when the song ended I looked over at him again.

"Aren't you gonna ask me my name?"

"I already know your name Larissa. I found that shit out as soon as I laid eyes on you. I'm not gonna bullshit you. I own this club ma. I got it like that, but I'm not a nigga to sit and brag about shit that's irrelevant. I'm feeling you and I can tell you feeling my ass too."

"I don't know you. So what makes you think you're having any kind of effect on me. Shit we barely even said two words to each other. Now you're claiming shit."

As soon as I said that shit, he moved his chair so that it was angled in front of mine now instead of just by the side. While I was trying to figure out what he was doing I felt his hand on my pussy. He really had slipped his hand under my exposed thigh and done that shit. Since my legs were crossed he had easy access to my pussy. The thong I was wearing did little to keep his hand from moving them to the side.

Then I felt his finger enter me moving it in and out of my pussy a few times. I tried to play the shit off like I wasn't enjoying it. But my body was damn near trembling and my breathing had even sped up. I looked over where Shanice was and she was having a conversation with one of Antoine's niggas so her ass wasn't paying us any attention. I wasn't a hoe to be doing shit like this though no matter how good the shit felt, so I lifted up slightly off the seat and uncrossed my legs before switching legs that were crossed. In the process it closed off the access he had to my pussy. He squeezed my ass with his hand before completing moving it away.

"I only speak on shit I know Larissa. Your pussy was tight and dripping wet from me being close to your ass."

"Whatever nigga and don't try that shit again. I'm not one of these nasty hoes out here that will do anything for a fine nigga or a few dollars. If you know about me like you say then you would know that already."

He nodded his head and turned his attention to the VIP section he had come out of. There was a nigga standing in the section who gave Antoine a head nod. Not two minutes later that same man had another nigga in his face in what looked like a heated argument. They were all the way across the club but from what I could see more men were getting involved and the shit looked like it was escalating.

"Go home. I'll get up with you tomorrow."

He didn't have to tell my ass twice. I wasn't trying to be caught up in no crazy shit and when mothafuckas started arguing at the club I was well aware that bullets often followed. I wasn't at the club much but I heard about the shit that seemed to happen every weekend. I rushed to get Shanice's attention and we both moved fast as hell out the side exit door to leave.

After stopping by the Waffle House for some food we made it back to Shanice's house and crashed. I fell asleep thinking about another man besides Messiah for the first time ever.

I wondered how and if Antoine would get up with me anyway. There was definitely something that drew me to him and the way my pussy was soaking wet from his touch had me horny for someone other than Messiah which was surprising too.

Messiah (Money)

I just got back in town a day ago and although it was good to be back, having to be around LaLa and not being her man was already proving to be hard as hell. Especially with the way her ass was looking and then knowing she was out all night had me all in my feelings today.

My dick was the only one that felt them walls but I had to accept that Larissa was a beautiful woman who wasn't mine anymore. It was only a matter of time before she met another nigga and gave up the goods, and I shouldn't even feel some way about the shit. I was fucking other bitches the whole time I was in Belize and even now but it was easier said than done dealing with that shit. I would continue to remind myself that her life was on the line messing with my ass. So even though shit was hard, it was still better than the alternative.

Silk and me were riding through the hood because I needed to check on how shit was going. I was still a hands on nigga when it came to our drug shit and definitely with our legit businesses. On a typical day I would spend at least fourteen hours working if not more. I lived for this shit and I wasn't nowhere near satisfied with where I was at on either front.

Silk and Draco had been holding things down while I was gone but mothafuckas needed to see the boss was back. I missed riding through the hood daily and being away from my niggas. Belize was straight but it wasn't home. I would love to visit regularly and knew when I took over everything I would be back and forth a lot. But as a full time residence I needed to be in the U.S.

Our shipments increased tenfold since making the deal with my father. We set up a team in Miami too. They were already doing business with the family cartel but now I was who they answered to instead of Emeri. I had to admit it seemed like he really put a lot of trust in me and it almost made me want to reconsider taking his ass out. But I peeped the sneaky shit he did too while I was down there.

He always held private meetings with various drug lords and cartel bosses from Columbia and Mexico without me being present. Sometimes he did request my presence but I paid attention to the shit that happened on the side too.

Over the past eight months I was able to get Emeri's moves down like clockwork. I met with all his business associates and worked directly with the entire crew in Belize. I was confident that the takeover would be possible. Of course I had to off his ass but I wasn't losing no sleep over that shit. He didn't give a fuck about me my whole life until he realized I was a boss out here. So fuck him.

Even though the weather was mild for this time of the year having just got back from a tropical fucking paradise this shit felt cold to me. We pulled up to one of our traps on the Eastside. The one I first took over. Miko's ass was standing out front looking crazy as hell with his arms folded and mean mugging not a damn thing. He was literally standing there ready to fuck some shit up probably for no damn reason and it was too dark to really see shit anyway. He stayed ready whether it was day or night. I had to give him that so I couldn't say shit.

"What's up boss?" He called out as I approached.

"Shit just touched down yesterday and gotta make sure everything good nigga."

"You already know we on top of it. Ain't nothing to worry 'bout."

"That's what I like to hear. Good looking out. What's the word on the street 'bout the trap on Randall?"

I was trying to get information on one of our other spots on the Eastside. From what Silk told me numbers had been low. Nothing was coming up short and our team swore up and down they didn't know why shit had slowed down. The amount was barely noticeable, but I was all about the fucking money. I could have let it go since we had plenty of money coming in and were expanding to other states but this was my hometown. It was important that everything was A1 on our home turf so niggas understood that we really was on top of everything and not slipping in any way.

"Some new niggas opened up shop. They copping from a connect that make their shit competitive with ours. They on the North Side but the niggas making moves. They got some major protection from the Italians from what I heard so ain't nobody trying to go against them."

"I see. Well we gonna have to change that."

"It's whatever on our end boss. But there's more. My nigga knows one of the boys they got running for them and he overheard your brother's name."

After getting a little more info from Miko about what he knew about them niggas who were trying to move in on our city I left mad as fuck. Not only were they doing business without the shit coming through our operation but the fact that my brother's name came up in conversation couldn't be a fucking coincidence. I had been on the lookout for information about the snitch who sold my brother out to feds for the past two years.

All this shit made my mood completely do a one eighty. It was time to focus a hundred percent on business and getting shit taken care of. First with the niggas in town and then taking over my father's cartel.

Right now though I couldn't complain too much about the way things was going between my father's cartel and me. The Aranda name alone held a lot of power not only in Belize but everywhere. Mothafuckas in the drug world knew that my father's cartel worked hand in hand with the Los Zetas gang out of Mexico and provided a key transport point in bringing narcotics in from South America to the States. I learned the inner workings of the routes and met with all the main players when I was studying behind my father for the past six months.

I was able to learn more about the marijuana fields that were part of my father's cartel too. That was how he originally rose to power in Belize. I had to give it to the mothafucka he might have fucked up as a parent but when it came to the drug game he had shit on lock and was smart as hell with how he set shit up.

I couldn't make what I was about to do personal though. To me Emeri was just another nigga stupid enough to trust the next man when he should have known better. There was a reason he waited so long to bring me into the family too. I wasn't dumb enough to think he didn't have some kind of ulterior motive.

It was already around 1 a.m. and I still wanted to drop by Carina's spot and see Monae. Ever since LaLa put the possibility in my head about her not being my daughter I started to question shit. Especially now that I had my son who looked just like my twin. I saw pictures of

Monae while I was gone and I couldn't find any resemblence to my features or anyone in my family anywhere. She did look a lot like Carina which is why I originally let it slide. But I was gonna get that DNA test tonight if I had my way.

I didn't bother sending Carina's ass a text or calling before pulling up. It shouldn't matter anyway since I was the one paying all the bills at her spot. Carina was content to sit around and collect money from me like I owed her something. When I got to the front door I heard voices from inside her townhouse. I didn't give a fuck who Carina chose to be around but there wasn't no way she was gonna bring random bitches or niggas around Monae. At least not until I got the DNA results and found out if she was mine or not.

I went ahead and pulled my pistol out and held it at my side while I knocked on the door. Carina eventually opened the door and instantly her expression let me know her ass was worried. Her eyes got big and she looked behind her then right back at me all nervous and shit.

"Hey Money what you doing here?"

"What you mean what I'm doing here? Stop fucking around Carina. Open the damn door. I wanna see Monae and I got some shit to take care of."

I said referring to the at home DNA test I had in my pocket. I bought that shit and was damn sure about to put it to use. There wasn't no problem with me claiming and loving Monae. But I wasn't gonna take care of another nigga's responsibility either and be out here being played by Carina's ass.

"Well I'm busy. You can't show up and expect me to let you in when your ass been gone for months nigga. Monae's asleep anyway, so get up with me tomorrow."

She was really trying to get rid of me because she even started to close the door. But before she could get it closed all the way I stuck my foot out and caught it. I pushed past her and walked into the shit like I owned the place, since I technically did.

I wanted to see who her ass had over here that she was scared I was gonna see. Something was definitely up. I walked in her living room, then kitchen and finally in the bedrooms and bathrooms. I even checked under the beds and in the closets. There wasn't a trace of anyone else in the place.

But I knew what the fuck I heard. So I figured whoever was here made an escape while Carina was stalling me. I was pretty sure it was a nigga's voice I heard and sooner or later I would find out why her ass was trying to hide his identity so bad. I finally stepped back into the living room where Carina was already sitting on one of her chairs. She was looking at her pedicured nails like she didn't give a fuck about me searching her damn house but I knew she was shook.

"You find whatever the fuck you're lookin' for Money?" I chose to ignore her question and pulled out the DNA test while I looked her dead in the eyes.

"What the fuck is that? You denying your daughter now! You had a baby by that bitch and now it's fuck Monae! I don't think so nigga, you not 'bout to try this shit with me."

She was screaming but I didn't give a fuck. I was gonna get the test done no matter what.

"Go get Monae and bring her out here Carina. I'm not here to listen to your fuckin' mouth."

"I'm not doing shit nigga! That's MY baby and I ain't got to do a goddamn thing!" I aimed the pistol right at her ass knowing she was gonna change her tune real quick.

"Like I said go get her." She gave me the nastiest look but knew better than to say some more slick shit.

She really was trying me since she first opened the door. I didn't have much patience left and she already knew how pushing my buttons wasn't smart. I didn't tolerate disrespect. I stayed calm so far because I had a mission to accomplish and that was more important.

Monae had grown a lot while I was away. She looked more like a toddler than a damn baby. She was cute for sure but whether or not she was really mine was all that mattered at the moment. Carina sat next to me with the baby on her lap facing me. I opened the test kit and used the swabs to collect some samples from Monae. Carina started crying being all dramatic while I was doing the shit too. The way she was carrying on really had me questioning whether the baby was mine or not even more than I was before. Why would she care so much about the test if Monae was mine?

I leaned over and kissed Monae on the cheek and then left out of the house. I wasn't trying to spend time with Carina and I wanted to get the test sent off first thing in the morning. So I went ahead and drove right to the post office to drop it in the mail. It said the results would come back in after a couple weeks.

Carina

I was so fuckin' pissed off that Money pulled that shit yesterday. First he decided to drop by unannounced after being out of the picture altogether for months. To make the shit so bad he almost caught me with another nigga too.

Torio was basically living with me for the last few weeks. As soon as Money pushed past me he had his damn gun pulled out ready for some shit to go down. His ass thought I had someone over because me and Torio was arguing right before he knocked on the door.

The worst part was I knew Money wasn't mad about me possibly fucking with someone else. He was mad because he was paying all my bills and this was really his place on top of the fact that Monae was living here. He didn't play when it came to disrespect or his child.

Which was so funny to me too since he was acting all overprotective but his ass wanted to get a DNA test for our baby. I was nervous about the results too because I did slip up a few times with my tricks I was fucking with at the time. I was being real reckless with my actions around that time so really there was no telling who Monae's father was. If it came back and Money wasn't the father I knew he would be more than done with my ass. Not only would he put us out but he was a dangerous nigga who might kill my ass for real.

I couldn't spend time worrying about that shit now though. I had some more shit I was into that would definitely make him kill my ass even if the other shit didn't. Torio called earlier and told me it was time for us to put the new plan he had come up with in motion.

I really wasn't with the shit he wanted to do but he won me over when I found out Larissa's bitch ass was involved. That weak ass hoe got lucky last time in Miami and recovered from the shooting. This time I was gonna make sure she suffered before I killed her ass. As soon as she came in the picture shit went bad for me and she needed to pay for it.

Torio did some fucked up shit to me over the time we were together. One day he would treat me like I meant the world to him and then the next day he would do the most fucked up shit. It had gotten to the point where he became violent and would slap my ass around but the fucked up part was I liked it just as much as hated it. That's why I was sticking with him. Me and him were just alike and I realized that we really were meant for each other. He convinced me to move back to NC and now here we were about to finally get revenge on that bitch and Money's ass too.

Larissa

Messiah or should I say Money had been back in town for about a month and the more time that passed the easier it was becoming to be around his ass. He kept MJ every other weekend and one night during the week. At first it was hard for me to let MJ go and be away from me for even a short amount of time. But I knew in the long run it was better for him to have a close relationship with his father. It was important that a child have both their parents in their life and I wanted nothing but the best for him.

Since the night at the club when me and Shanice went out I was a hundred percent on my grind when it came to school. Summer classes were starting soon and I already added some classes on top of what I initially registered for. It was even more than I was technically allowed to take. But two of them were partial online courses which gave me more time to get coursework complete.

On top of school, Antoine had also captured some of my attention. He called me the very next day after meeting like he said he would. It turned out he knew my brother and that was how he knew who I was at the club. He came clean about that shit when we talked on the phone that first day. Which I was glad about because I didn't want him to know me because of Money's ass. I didn't trust many people as it was but little by little he was earning some from me.

He also made it a point to treat me really well. Twice a week he took me out or we went on a date doing something. It was usually something exciting or different. I honestly never had someone treat me the way he did. Not that Messiah didn't treat me good or love me, but Antoine treated me more like a woman. I felt like what we were hopefully building was some grown ass real shit.

The love I had for Messiah would always be there but it felt like it was a lifetime ago and I was a completely different person now. I grew and changed so much since last year it wasn't even funny.

Messiah was on his way over to pick MJ up for the weekend and I was packing for a weekend trip with Antoine. He was taking me to the mountains for the weekend and the thought alone had me getting all hot and bothered. I had a feeling that this weekend we would definitely have sex and I couldn't wait. It had been so long since I felt a man and Antoine always made me feel so good with his touch. Just as I was thinking about the possibilities of the weekend my doorbell rang.

I went ahead and checked on MJ who was in his playpen before making my way to the door. Like I figured Messiah was at the door. I went ahead and let him in and then went into my room to grab MJ's bag for him. For some reason Messiah's ass followed me into my room and stood there looking at me like he had some shit to say.

Messiah never was one to hold back when he had some shit to say so I was kind of caught off guard. Whenever he picked up MJ he always stayed in the living room too and we never really held a conversation either so the whole thing was weird as hell.

"So you really feeling that nigga huh?"

"Messiah I'm not doing this with you." I said in a sincere voice.

I didn't want to discuss my personal life with my ex whatsoever. Messiah was the one who left me and I had moved on. Now I was starting a relationship with another man and wasn't about to let him back in, not even a little bit. Not even on the friend tip. I just wanted us to be able to co-parent. That was it.

"LaLa you're always gonna be mine. Your pussy always gonna be mine too. Remember that shit."

"Whatever Money. You have no right to sit here and say shit to me. This…" I said pointing between us like he had done before, "This is over, been over. You do you, and I'm damn sure gonna do me nigga. I always will have love for you but I'm trying to be happy and move on."

"You got that then." He said before turning around and leaving out mad as hell.

I couldn't believe this nigga had the nerve to not only come over here and question me and act jealous but try and act like I was doing something wrong by moving on. He was the one who left me. He was the one who almost caused me to lose mine and our child's life and then threw our relationship away afterwards.

I wasn't even gonna waste any more of my time trying to figure out the reasoning behind the shit he did. My life was moving in the right direction and I was smiling again. There wasn't no way I was gonna revert back to the place I was at when he broke me down.

A text came through on my phone a few minutes later from Antoine letting me know he was downstairs. So I turned off the lights, grabbed my suitcase and walked downstairs where Antoine was waiting. It was time to really move forward and let another man into my life.

Messiah (Money)

I fucked up and let Larissa go and now I was sitting here feeling sick over the shit. It was like I couldn't be with her ass and I couldn't be without her either. It was times like this that I wish I had never even laid eyes on her in the first place. But then I immediately caught myself thinking about all the good times we shared and how real the love and bond was that we had.

Even now I felt like she was connected to me and not just because we shared a son, but because our spirits were like one in the same. I had hurt her and so for right now she was right we needed to stay in our separate lanes. If shit was meant to be then later on in life maybe we would end up back together, maybe not. I needed to stay focused on all the other bullshit I had going on anyway.

The other fucked up part was LaLa was fucking around with the nigga Antoine that was moving into our territory. So far he hadn't pressed any further and was staying up north so we weren't doing shit for now. Not to mention he had some kind of connection to my brother. I hadn't been to visit my brother since he had been in but now I needed to have a face to face conversation and see what the deal was as far as that cat was concerned.

Malik never talked about anything street related over the prison phones, not even in coded talk. He believed the feds were always paying attention and didn't want to be caught slipping or be the reason why one of us on the outside got jammed up either.

This Antoine nigga was stepping on our toes in the streets and now he was getting real close to my fucking heart, LaLa. So I needed as much information on him as possible. Even though he didn't like anyone to visit I pulled some strings and got his ass moved a few hours away so the drive wasn't too bad. I dropped MJ with my mama for a few hours and planned on picking him up on my way back from the visit.

When I arrived I went through the typical protocol and made it through security. I didn't have any felonies so visiting really wasn't a problem and we took care of all the paperwork right after he was processed and transferred. When I walked into the visiting room my brother was already sitting at a table and after greeting each other with a hug we sat down.

"What's up Messiah? I'm glad to see your ass but you know I don't do the visiting shit, so it must be important."

"What you know 'bout a nigga named Antoine?" I saw a look of surprise cross my brother's face that was quickly replaced with his usual unreadable expression.

"On some real shit I met his ass right before I got locked up. Turns out we all got the same father or some shit and the nigga is our half-brother. He's from New York and some of our cousins from up there put two and two together."

I sat there for a minute thinking about the shit my brother was telling me. The story he was telling me seemed fucking unbelievable but I knew he wasn't bullshitting me. Malik always kept shit one hundred and that was what was fucking with me most. The fact that he didn't think to tell me we had a brother out there was some questionable shit to begin with.

Now this nigga who happens to be my half-brother sets up shop in NC while I'm in Belize and is now fucking with Larissa. That shit seemed like too much of a fucking coincidence. I wasn't buying it for a minute.

"Why didn't you tell me this shit before I had to come and ask your ass?"

"Look little bruh there's more to it than you think. Antoine didn't know 'bout us either. Seems like our father wasn't in his life either. I wanted to talk with ma first before I brought this to you and Maurice. But right after I found out the feds came so I didn't get a chance."

"His ass is in NC now and becoming a fuckin' problem." I told him straight up.

"All I'm gonna say is talk to his ass before you make any moves. Shit might not be what you think. I know your hot headed ass and I don't want you doing something you gon' regret later."

I gave my brother a dirty ass look because everything he was saying right now was pissing me the fuck off even more. I decided to just go ahead and change the subject since there wasn't nothing else for us to discuss about that nigga. I was gonna take care of the situation the way I saw fit and no mothafucka not even Malik could sway the decisions I made.

He may have been my older brother, the one who gave me a start but I was the boss of this shit. At the end of the day I would always love and have respect for him but that didn't have nothing to do with how I conducted business.

We ended our visit a little while later not even staying for the whole four hours. It was good as hell to see my bro but he would rather me stay away so that I didn't get caught up either. After saying our goodbyes I made my way out of the camp and hit the road trying to get back to the city as soon as possible.

It was my weekend to have MJ and I had dropped him off with my mama so I could make the trip to see Malik. I always loved keeping my lil man. He really was like my fucking twin and being able to take care of him was the highlight of my life right now besides making money.

When I pulled up to my mama's house I was surprised to see all the lights still on inside the house since it was damn near midnight. I let myself in and walked into the kitchen where my mama was sitting at the kitchen table smoking a cigarette. She only smoked when she was stressed out so I knew something was up.

"Ma what's up? Everything good with MJ?" I asked.

"Your father called today and asked me to meet him tomorrow. I haven't seen him in over twenty years Messiah. I know you think your father didn't want nothing to do with ya'll but that wasn't the case. I left him." She said the last part quiet as hell.

My mother was never quiet about anything. She always said what was on her mind, and I thought never kept shit from us. I guess I was wrong. But no matter what she raised us the best she could and I knew she had her reasons for what she did. I wasn't about to sit up here and feel some type of way towards my mama. I wasn't built like a bitch ass nigga who could ever be mad at my mama no matter what.

"It's all good. I ain't worried 'bout that man. He could have been in our lives if he wanted to and that's on him. I got no love for him. You can meet with him if you want. But don't feel obligated to do nothing if you don't want."

"I love you son." She said while wiping a tear away from her face. Changing the subject she spoke up saying, "You got some mail today too. I think it's the test results for Monae."

I still got most of my personal mail at my mom's house on purpose so if we got picked up not all of my shit would be searched. The feds could still pull out all the stops if they wanted to, but most likely they wouldn't think to if they didn't need to.

I took the envelope that my mother was holding out for me. I immediately ripped it open and read the results of the paternity test I sent off a few weeks ago. I was hurt by the shit I was reading but felt in my heart that it was for the best. I loved that little girl, but she wasn't mine. Carina's ass was out there hoeing around it turned out and tried to play me.

That shit had me on ten ready to murder her ass. At the same time I was relieved that I wasn't gonna have to deal with her for the next eighteen years. Larissa crossed my mind too and the fact that now she really was the only woman who had my child. But I guess that shit didn't matter since we wasn't together anyway.

Larissa

This weekend turned out to be perfect so far. Last night me and Antoine cooked a dinner together after stopping by the store on our way here. While we were cooking that shit took a turn to being something more sexual with him eating my pussy right on the damn kitchen counter. We didn't take it any further than oral sex and I didn't even return the favor. I was ready for us to take it to the next level and wanted the dick so bad. It had been over a year since I had sex and my body was craving the feeling to the max.

I was pretty sure tonight would be the night. As I stood in the bathroom mirror adjusting my shirt and jeans that I picked out for the day, I couldn't help but admire my reflection. I finally lost most of the baby weight I had been carrying since having MJ. My ass and breasts were still bigger than they used to be but for the most part my stomach was back to being flat and toned. I had been working out every day and overall I was happy with the results.

I wanted to call and check on MJ before I started my day. Messiah was really doing a good job with him and MJ seemed to love his ass more than me sometimes. I even found myself getting a touch of jealously with how strong their bond was after his ass was MIA for the first few months. But really I couldn't ask for more from Messiah.

He was a great father if nothing else and things between us were getting better also. Except for when he tried to check me for the shit I was getting into with Antoine. I dialed up Messiah's number and knew his ass was sound asleep as soon as he answered from his voice.

"Yo, LaLa. What's up?"

"How's my baby doing?"

Messiah turned face time on and I was able to see my chunky little man laying right next to his ass in bed. Every time I saw my son I couldn't help but smile. He really made me complete. MJ was still fast asleep so I decided to end the call. Before I got a chance to disconnect or turn the camera off, Antoine walked in the bedroom and Messiah saw that shit.

Messiah automatically woke all the way up and then turned off face time so we were on a regular call again.

"I'm telling you right now. You better not fuck that nigga Larissa. On God."

"Whatever Money." I said right back to his ass before I quickly hung up the phone.

I didn't want to hear nothing he had to say. He had absolutely no right to continue with the jealous shit he was on. A part of me was feeling glad that he was getting a taste of his own medicine, but I really wasn't moving forward with Antoine to make him mad. I was starting to care about him and the truth was I had been lonely over the past year.

More than that Antoine treated me like a queen and I was starting to be happier than I had been in a long time. I definitely wasn't about to let Messiah mess that up for me. Messiah sent me a few texts warning me. But I knew his ass wasn't about to do nothing to me. He walked away from me and that was all there was to it.

After we were finished getting ready for the day Antoine and I headed out to find some of the waterfalls in the area. We both didn't want to go on a long ass hike or anything. But we were adventurous enough to see what was out there at least. We were able to see a couple not too far off the road before we headed back to the lodge we were staying at for lunch.

On the drive back Antoine's hand rested on my thigh and he was caressing it which had become normal for us whenever I rode with him anywhere. I was still horny from last night and decided to make a move. I reached over into his lap while he was driving and began to rub on his dick through his pants. He had a big ass dick. Probably about the same size as Messiah's and the thought alone had my mouth and pussy watering. That's how bad I was in need of some dick.

"You keep that shit up we not even gonna make it back to the house."

"Oh yeah?" I asked in a challenging way. I was ready for everything he was gonna do to me.

He just looked over at me not saying another damn word and then turned back towards the road. He sped the car up so that we were driving at least 70 over the mountain roads. We made it back to the lodge in record time and hurried our way into the house.

I literally hopped out and started jogging while looking over my shoulder and laughing. Antoine was on my ass though and before I could even open the front door he had me pinned against it. He lifted me up so my legs were wrapped around him while we were kissing each other with a hunger. Somehow he managed to open the door and then set my ass down. He looked me dead in the eyes and said with a tone that sent a chill down my spine.

"Once I feel that pussy you're mine. I hope you're ready 'cus I'm 'bout to fuck up your life."

I looked right back at him and said, "What you waiting for then?"

He lifted my ass up and carried me upstairs like it was nothing with his hands on my ass the whole time. Once inside the bedroom he laid me on the bed and started getting undressed. I did the same only leaving my thong and bra on. I sat up some so I could see what he was working with.

Antoine's dick was big as hell and already hard. I went ahead and made my way over to him and got down on my knees.

I wanted to show him how much I appreciated him. I grabbed his dick and began stroking it up and down while licking his shaft. I looked up and saw him staring down at me. I went ahead and continued to go to work. I let his dick slide down all the way into the back of my throat and began bobbing my head up and down letting spit come down and coat his dick even more. I knew he was liking the head I was giving him because he began to fuck my mouth back.

He was still watching me and I wanted to really put on a show for his ass so I began to use my other hand to play with my pussy moving my thong to the side. He used his hand on the back of my head to apply more pressure. So I picked up the pace as I felt his body tense up. Before he could cum I pulled away. I was ready to feel him inside me.

I stood up and he grabbed ahold of me roughly before turning me around and unhooking my bra then sliding my panties down. I stepped out of them one leg at a time bending over so he had a full view of my pussy from the back. He slapped me on the ass and then told me to get on the bed. I walked over to the bed and laid down spreading my legs wide.

He didn't waste any time coming over and positioning himself between my legs. He leaned down and started sucking on my neck, breasts and using his fingers to stretch my pussy. I knew he was getting me ready for his big ass dick, but I was beyond ready to feel him inside me. He finally gave me what I wanted and worked his dick in inch by inch.

My pussy clenched down on his shit right away. I was tight as hell from not having sex in so long and made a loud ass moan. Once I adjusted to his size he began to fuck me nice and slow with deep strokes. I was having a hard time matching his rhythm because with every stroke I was on the brink of cumming. It felt so good.

It had been so long since I experienced some good ass dick. But before I had a chance to cum Antoine flipped me around so that I was on top. I planted my feet on either side of him and began bouncing up and down on his dick taking it all the way in each time I came down.

"Ride that shit out Larissa."

I continued to do my thing and began to go even harder with Antoine fucking me from underneath.

"Shit, I'm 'bout to cum. Fuck!" I shouted out.

My body started shaking and my juices flowed out soaking everything. Antoine grabbed my hips and turned me around so that I was on all fours before he started eating my pussy from the back. He was licking and slurping and the shit felt so good I let my body go and started backing my ass up more.

He surprised me when he stopped and replaced his mouth with his dick. I screamed out and was already about to cum again. He held onto my hips and started fucking me rough as hell. This shit felt so good almost like the way Messiah fucked me.

Damn my head was fucked up I thought. I pushed the thought of Messiah to the back of my mind and focused back on the feelings Antoine was giving me.

"Take the dick, don't fuckin' move."

"I can't take it no more." I said back.

Antoine continued to dig as deep as he could. I felt him in my damn stomach and then he tensed up. I had been holding back from cumming like he told me to and was damn near in pain from the shit.

"Let that shit go." Antoine whispered in my ear.

We both cummed at the same time and as soon as my senses came back to me I realized that I had really done it. I had been with another man besides Messiah and guilt started taking over.

I don't know why I felt guilty when he was most definitely having his share of hoes that he was fucking with. But I just never thought I would be with another man when we were together. I also didn't use a condom with Antoine which was not something I wanted to make a habit of. I didn't know if he was clean and didn't want to risk my life over a nigga I had only known for a month or so. I was at least on birth control so I wasn't worried about getting pregnant.

After our sex session we both took turns in the shower getting ready. I was pretty sure Antoine could tell something was off. He asked me about it once when we were getting back dressed, but I reassured him that I was good. I told him the sex tired me out since it had been so long and kind of fucked with my head since I had only been with one man before. He said he understood but I wasn't so sure he did. He seemed to get pissed off and by the time night came around we were barely speaking to each other.

Shit I was honest with his ass and I wasn't gonna sit here trying to boost his ego because he wanted to be all in his feelings. I wasn't a woman who chased after a man no matter what. The way he was acting wasn't only a turn off it was making me question whether we were really compatible to begin with. I needed a man who would boss up on my ass when needed, not cower away.

Finally, I asked him to just take me home and told him it was better if we end the getaway early. He didn't say shit about it and basically gave my ass the silent treatment the whole ride home which was over five hours. By the time he pulled into my complex I was even more pissed off.

What started out as something not that serious had turned into a big fucking deal all because he wanted me to act more emotionally into us. I just wasn't there, especially after having sex. Not because the sex wasn't good, but because my head was still fucked up behind Messiah's ass and I couldn't even help it if I wanted to. I did care about Antoine that's why I even went as far as I did with him. But this shit he pulled was definitely not helping our relationship.

"I guess I'll see you when I see you."

"Whatever Antoine. I don't even know why you're acting like this." I said right back to his ass since he was really pissing me off.

"You got a nigga out here open and you don't appreciate that shit shorty. When you get your shit together holla at me."

I stared right back at him while he said the last part. I guess he did have a point. My anger at Antoine started to fade some. I still thought he could have handled the situation differently but he was speaking the truth. I was acting fucked up and that was on me. I leaned over and kissed him deep and slow.

"I appreciate it all." I said low before getting out of the car. I meant that shit too. Antoine had been treating me like a queen and fucked me good. He fucked me better than good actually, but I couldn't seem to shake the funk

I was in. Maybe he was right I needed to get my shit together for real.

Antoine waited for me to walk inside my apartment before he pulled away. It was the little things like that which made me see how much he really cared about me. Most niggas wouldn't give a fuck after how things went down between us. As soon as I walked in my apartment I was met with two hands pushing me up against the wall.

The lights were off so I couldn't get a good look at who it was. I started to scream but the intruder put his hand up to my mouth before a sound came out. I instantly knew I had fucked up.

Messiah (Money)

When the love of your fucking life entertains another nigga there's no telling what it will have you doing. As soon as Larissa walked through the door I rushed her ass and was almost ready to kill her. I could smell that nigga scent on her and it was making me sick.

My LaLa, my damn wife had been with another man. She let another nigga feel what was mine and that crushed me.

I stood with her pressed against the wall for a few minutes before I finally regained my composure. There was no way I was gonna kill her because I was the one who let her go, but it still was hard as fuck to fully accept that shit.

While I was holding onto her I felt the moment she recognized it was me. My body responded to her even though my mind was fucked up. My dick was hard as hell and ready to feel my pussy. Which wasn't my pussy anymore. Damn.

I backed away and went over to the living room still leaving the apartment pitch black. I heard Larissa's footsteps come behind me and she went ahead and turned on the lights. I sat down on the couch and made sure to stare her ass down with a mean ass mug. She sat down on the chair across from me and looked right back at my ass like she was just as fucked up as I was about the shit she had done. After our stare off she finally spoke up first like I knew she would.

"Really Messiah? You break in here and put your hands on me. And over what? The fact I moved on? I moved on because YOU left ME!"

"I told your ass not to fuck that nigga." I replied right back to her ass.

"What I do is none of your business. You fucked me over. Don't you get it? I gave my heart to you completely thinking we was gonna share a lifetime and you left me nigga. On my deathbed while I was fighting for my life you said fuck me. What did you think was gonna happen? That I was gonna be alone for the rest of my life?"

"I don't know. Damn. But this shit hurts. I fucking love you. Will always love you but it's always been best if I'm not with you. I gotta keep you safe. Now you go and fuck that nigga, my own fucking brother. What the hell is wrong with you? Out here being a hoe, not worried about your son and shit."

"Fuck you!" Larissa screamed at my ass.

She was crying and doing the most but I was the one going through it now over the shit she was doing.

She got up and ran to her bedroom while I followed right behind her ass. She was laying on the bed face down when I came in the room and I started to feel bad for how I talked to her. She didn't know he was my brother. She didn't' know why I stayed away after she was shot. That was on me, it was my fault because I never said shit to her about it.

I walked over and looked down at the woman I loved laying there crying because of me and felt like shit. I bent down and started rubbing on her back. I wanted to make her feel better at least for a little while. I moved my hands from her back down to her ass. I knew she had been with another nigga but she was still mine and always would be no matter what. I gripped her ass and pulled her leggings off. She didn't object or even look back up at me so I kept going.

I stepped out of my pants and thought about eating her pussy, but couldn't even do that shit knowing she probably let that nigga taste her too. Shit I was just gonna fuck and then bounce. My head was all fucked up.

I let my dick slide in and her pussy still felt tight. I was in damn heaven with how her shit was gripping my dick. I grabbed her hips and pulled her back into me and whispered into her ear.

"You see how your pussy fit my dick. Already fuckin' wet you better remember who the fuck I am."

Larissa didn't say nothing back but she didn't have to her body was telling me everything we both already knew. Her moans were filling the room and the thought alone of her fucking another nigga and giving away what was only meant for me had me fucking her even harder. Shit I needed to punish her ass for letting that nigga feel this shit.

I put one hand down on her back to keep her from trying to move while she was bent over the side of the bed. Her ass was trying to run from the dick but I wasn't havin' that. With my other hand I grabbed ahold of her hips and pulled her back further into me. It was like I was trying to dig as deep as I could and make it so she never forgot the feeling only I could give her. Instead of LaLa taking her punishment she started fucking me back working her pussy muscles even more squeezing my dick. She was hollaring out all types of shit.

"Yes Messiah! I love it."

"Damn right now turn around." I told her.

She went ahead and turned around as I pulled my dick out of her and held the big mothafucka in my hand. I felt all her cum and juices that were on it which made me smile at her ass. I bet that nigga wasn't fucking her like I was or had her ass doing any and every thing I did. Shit it didn't matter anyway I was gonna leave my damn mark and then let that nigga know what was up before I killed his ass anyway. Wasn't no way he was about to live after this shit.

Larissa was staring up at me with an impatient look like she couldn't wait to have my dick filling her up again. So I lifted her ass up and let her legs wrap around my waist before I sat down and let her ride the monster. Since she wanted it so bad I was gonna let her show me how much.

I kept my hands on her ass cheeks while she began bouncing up and down with her titties in my face. I slid a finger in her ass and that sent her in a fucking craze. She was going harder than before and once she squirted all over my shit I released a big fucking nut right in her. Her pussy was mine anyway and I would love for her ass to get pregnant right away. Even though her ass was probably on birth control like she told me she was gonna be.

After we were done fucking there was an awkwardness in the room. Neither one of us said shit to the other and that was something we never had done. Even when we went through all the other bullshit we did in the past we never held our tongues or kept shit from each other. The thing was I knew I wasn't trying to be in a relationship with Larissa right now. The fact was it was still safer for her if we weren't together. Plus she just got into a relationship with another nigga, my brother at that and that fucked me up in the head.

It may have been fucked up that I could fuck all the bitches I wanted but for her to fuck a nigga showed me she had feelings for his ass. I didn't have no feelings for none of the women I fucked. They were just there to satisfy my needs nothing more. I knew LaLa well enough to know there was no way she would have sex with a man and not care about him. She wasn't built like that.

"So what does this mean Messiah?" Larissa finally got the nerve up to ask after we were dressed.

I ran my hand through my dreads and then looked back at her. Us having sex was one thing, and when I looked at her I felt nothing but love. But she also betrayed me.

"You know your mine. But I'm not gonna lie to you. That shit with ol' boy got me fucked up. It's better if we just keep shit the way it was between us. I can't fuck with you like that right now."

"Really Messiah? You do everything under the fucking sun to me. Cheat on me, leave me, disrespect me and got the nerve to be in your feelings about one nigga I fucked? How does that make sense? You know what, forget this shit ever happened. You're absolutely right it's best if we stay the fuck away from each other."

I knew Larissa was hurt and I wanted to be able to go over to her and wipe her tears away again and make her feel better. But I just couldn't do that shit, my pride wouldn't allow me to. So instead I shrugged my shoulders and turned to leave.

Even as Larissa sat down on the bed with her hands covering her eyes crying I walked away. Shit was too fucked up for us right now to try and be together. If it was meant to be then we would work shit out eventually. But right now I didn't want to go down that road for the first time since I met her ass.

It was really time to be the heartless nigga I was before I got with Larissa. I was gonna grind even harder and stack my paper. Before all that though I was definitely gonna take care of the fuck nigga Antoine, brother or not.

Torio

It was time to finally to get at that bitch ass nigga Money. My uncle Emeri fucked up me and my pop's plans before, but this time I wasn't on his turf. He might have the capabilities to fuck shit up in the states but nothing like how he had shit on lock in Belize. He was a fucking king back there. Over here he was just one of the many bosses to worry about.

Since getting back in North Carolina I had been staying close to Carina for the simple fact that we had a mutual enemy. Money did the DNA test and found out that little girl wasn't his. Which made Carina even more ready to take his ass down. Shit she was ready and willing to do whatever the fuck I said. She was a crazy bitch and thought I really loved her ass which was funny as hell. I had a whole wife and family back home in Belize.

I hid them away right before all he shit went down with my uncle too. They were up in New York staying with some family on my mother's side. They couldn't stand my uncle Emeri either since they thought he was responsible for her death. So I knew they were safe with them.

I sat at a table outside of a restaurant located across the street from Money's business headquarters. I knew all about his operation including Money Makers Inc. The stupid mothafucka didn't even have a clue about how close he was to losing it all. He really was a cocky nigga and thought he was untouchable. He should have learned from last time, because I did. I wasn't about to let his ass get away this time. Especially since he had everything I wanted for myself.

Money had the business and drug game on lock. My uncle even took him under his wing when it should have been me that was being groomed to take over. I was a part of the family organization my whole fucking life and was built for the shit. Money came along out of nowhere and was about to run Belize and take over the East Coast. I wasn't about to let that shit happen no matter what. He also had the most loyal fine bitch I had come across. Larissa was worth ten of these other women out here and he didn't even give a fuck about her either. I was gonna show him how much he was really taking shit for granted and make him wish he was never born.

Money pulled up and parked in front of his office building. He looked stressed out and that shit had me wanting to laugh even more at his dumb ass. His niggas hopped out of the ride right after him and they all stood around for a minute chopping it up before parting ways and getting in their own whips. I needed to clock all their moves to make sure there was no loopholes in my plan. It was almost time but I needed to be patient so there wouldn't be no fuck ups this time.

Larissa

Things had gone back to normal or somewhat normal for me over the last month since fucking around with both Messiah and his brother Antoine. After that shit went down I decided to pull away from both of them and do some more soul searching.

Although I didn't know Antoine was Messiah's brother at the time I still wasn't trying to fuck with him for that fact alone. Not to mention I went ahead and had sex with Messiah right after. That let me know my feelings weren't gone for him. I wasn't about to be in a relationship with Antoine for that reason either.

I know it seemed like I left him hanging with not returning his calls and basically saying fuck him, but I didn't know how to tell him what I was feeling. He was a good man and hadn't done anything wrong. I truly didn't believe he knew Messiah was his brother and if he did then he would know why I wasn't fucking with him in the first place.

I started my summer classes and spent most of my waking hours going to class or studying if I wasn't tending to MJ. Even with my crazy ass class schedule I made sure to spend as much time as possible with my baby. It seemed like he was growing up too fast already. He would be a year old in a few months and was already trying to walk. MJ was the cutest too. His hair was thick as hell and he had the same eyes as his daddy which was bittersweet to me. I was always left thinking about Messiah's stupid ass when I looked at my son. It must have been my punishment or something.

My body was still craving sex to the max but I also realized that I wasn't one of those females that would fuck just to fuck. I needed to feel something and care about the man I had sex with. That left me feeling like I was doomed for the rest of my life. As foolish as that sounded it was how I felt.

Just as I was finishing putting the dishes away I heard my doorbell ring. I wasn't expecting anyone since it was Saturday morning and my weekend with MJ. Only a handful of people actually knew where I stayed though so I wasn't worried about who it could be. When I looked through the peephole I saw Shanice standing there with tears in her eyes and a crazy look.

I opened the door and let my best friend in. She rushed past me and automatically went to my kitchen. When I followed her I saw she had already gotten ahold of my red wine and was pouring us two glasses. It was only ten o'clock in the morning so I knew some shit was off if she was trying to sit here and have a glass of wine with me.

"What's up girl? Why we getting drunk this early?" I questioned as I sat my ass down.

So what if it was early as hell. If my best friend needed me and wanted to share a drink while she was going through something I damn sure was gonna be right there with her ass getting drunk. We were safe at home anyway.

"I think he's cheating on me. And I'm gonna kill that nigga!" Shanice said mad as hell.

"What makes you think that? Are you sure? Silk loves your ass and worships the ground you walk on." I reassured her.

"I'm telling you that nigga been acting strange as hell. He's been taking calls and walking out the room, being secretive as shit. He's also stopped answering when I call and something is telling me he's got another bitch. Call it woman's intuition." She said while gulping down the rest of her wine and pouring another glass.

"He might have good reason for how he's been acting. Sometimes what it seems like ain't what it really is." I replied speaking from experience.

I didn't know the real reasons behind Messiah breaking things off with me and that he was doing it to try and protect me. He still broke my heart and in my opinion should have been by my side when I needed him most. But I only knew what he allowed me to know. I knew how much Silk loved Shanice's ass and was really hoping there was a good explanation as to why he was acting shady as hell.

Shanice and I finished off the rest of the bottle of wine. We sat there coming up with plan to catch Silk doing whatever he was doing. We were gonna follow his ass around so Shanice could see firsthand what the deal was. I was still really buzzed even after showering and getting dressed. I went ahead and got MJ ready with the help of Shanice. What usually took a little while to give him a bath seemed to be the most complicated shit ever since we had drank that wine. After he was washed, dressed and fed I called up Ms. Sheila to see if she could come over and pick him up since I wasn't 'bout to have him ride with me after drinking even a little bit.

She agreed and made it over in fifteen minutes. We filled her in on what we were up to and she told us to take our time. She was more than supportive telling us we better catch his ass too if there was something going on. I could always count on Ms. Sheila for keeping it real and the way she was always there for me and MJ was more than I could asked for.

Shanice and I decided to get a rental for the day so Silk wouldn't be able to tell we were following him. He knew me and Shanice's rides and would for sure know we were up to some shit. Shanice called him and got him to tell her that he was on his way to the headquarters to handle some business. That was all she could get out of him though.

We made our way across town to Money Makers Inc. and pulled into a parking spot about a block away. We saw Silk, Draco and Messiah standing around in front for a few minutes until they each got back in their cars and started driving off.

I was driving with Shanice in the passenger seat smoking a blunt. The smoke from us burning was completely filling the car and would give someone a contact just from sitting in it. I followed behind Silk but there was a lot of traffic downtown which worked in our favor. He definitely wasn't able to tell we were tailing him. I felt like I was on some secret agent shit like one of those movies and I was doing a damn good job of following his ass too.

Silk ended up going past the high school we used to go to and past Shanice's parent neighborhood heading in the direction of the beach. He turned into a housing development soon after and Shanice stopped all the shit she had been talking immediately.

"It don't mean nothing yet honey." I said trying to help the situation.

It wasn't a good sign that he was turning into a place filled with nice houses. They were family type houses. Silk was in the drug game and supposedly doing business according to what he told Shanice so something was off.

Instead of replying to my comment Shanice threw the blunt out the window and continued staring straight ahead. I swear I could hear her damn heart beating over the music. Silk pulled in front of a nice two story home and I drove past with Shanice ducking down. Being extra cautious even though we had gotten a car with tinted windows.

I went ahead and turned down the next road and pulled up my GPS which showed the road looped back around to where Silk was parked. I followed it and then parked right behind him since he had already gone inside before we made it back to the spot. We were gonna stay right where we were until his ass came back out so we could really see what type of business he had going on.

Thirty minutes passed and Silk still hadn't come out so Shanice decided to just go ahead and knock on the door to see what was up. She was out of patience and I couldn't blame her. I really was doubting Silk at this point because this neighborhood just wasn't somewhere I had ever known Messiah to do business in either. He always took me with him on his rounds so I was just as skeptical of the shit as Shanice was.

No matter what I was gonna stand by my friend and be here for her if Silk really was pulling some shit. I knew too well how it felt to catch your nigga doing some scandalous shit. I was keeping a close eye on Shanice as she made her way over to the front of the house. My phone started ringing and I saw it was from Messiah. I hit ignore and then felt it vibrate indicting I had a message. He would have to wait. I knew if it was serious or had to do with MJ Ms. Sheila would be calling not Messiah's ass. He probably wanted to talk shit about how MJ was with his mother instead of me and call himself trying to check my ass anyway.

When I looked back up I hurried up and jumped out of the car to run over to where Shanice was.

Shanice

This was exactly why I didn't want to fuck with Silk's no good ass in the first place. Here I was following behind this nigga because he was up to no good. I felt it in my gut that he was fucking around on me. I had been in this situation before with my first love and got played. Now it was like dejavu all over again. I swore up and down that I wouldn't be dumb enough to let a nigga hurt me the same way, but here I was.

The worst part was that I was more in love with Silk than I ever thought possible. What I had with Andre was puppy love compared to the feelings I had for Silk. Kenneth was my everything and this shit right here was breaking my damn heart.

I was thankful to have Larissa by my side to see this shit though. There was no telling what I was gonna do when I actually caught his ass. When we turned in the neighborhood following behind his ass shit got more real. There was no other reason for him to be over here besides some shady shit. I wasn't a fool and I knew none of the business he had was out this way. Then he was taking a long ass time inside that fucking house. I was done waiting for his ass.

I walked right up to the door and knocked on it loud as hell like I was the damn police. Shit this situation called for way more than ringing the doorbell. I stood there waiting for the door to open with my hands on my hips. I was ready for war. Before the door was opened I heard a bitch yell out my nigga's name and his government at that which let me know she wasn't some random bitch either.

Silk opened the door and there wasn't a bitch in sight. I was glaring at his ass waiting for him to say something. But he didn't say shit. He just had a pitiful ass look on his face. I should have been the sad one, shit.

Since he wasn't saying anything I went ahead and tried to push past him into the house. I wasn't gonna waste my breath asking anything I was capable of seeing myself.

"Let me in nigga!" I yelled as he held me back from getting past him. I hadn't even stepped foot inside.

"Go home Shanice. Ain't shit here for you to see ma." Silk said calmly back to me with no fucking emotion whatsoever.

"Yeah bitch. Get the fuck away from my house. Kenneth take care of her." Some boujee looking model bitch said from behind him.

"Bitch? Who the fuck you calling bitch? I'm trying to figure out why MY nigga over here with your hoe ass. You don't want these problems." I let off.

The bitch started laughing before she turned around and walked back out of sight. I was really trying to break through past Silk at this point. I didn't let any bitch come out of their mouth sideways at me. This hoe really was in need of getting her ass beat. But there was no way I could get past his ass. He was too damn big. Larissa even got out the car and was trying to push his ass out of the way too so we could get by and beat that bitch down like she deserved.

"Like I said go home. I'll talk to you later." Silk said sounding out of breath from holding us back.

I stopped struggling with his ass and got enough composure to start walking away back towards the rental. Larissa started walking back with me with her arm around me. I turned back around and let him know it was over for us. There wouldn't be no talking. I saw what I needed to see and the rest was history.

"Fuck you Kenneth. I don't want to hear shit you got to say. Go get your bitch!"

Silk

Damn letting Shanice walk away was hard as hell. But I had to take care of Angela's ass first. I didn't know if Shanice and I would be together after this shit but there really wasn't nothing I could do about the situation I was in. I didn't like the shit one bit myself.

Angela and me had history together and she was my first girlfriend back in the day. We shared all our firsts together and she was the woman I thought was made for me. She came up in the same hood from nothing just like me and we naturally had a strong bond from that shit alone. Somewhere along the way she got caught up in all the money I started making and the lifestyle that came from being with a nigga like me. She lost sight of our relationship and started partying with her hoe ass friends more and more.

Angela was once my down ass bitch, but she turned into just another shallow hoe who only cared about shopping and gossip. It was like I didn't even recognize the girl I used to love. The shit got so bad between us that I was fucking everything in sight and Angela started fucking around on me too.

She knew I held too much love for her to put her out or kill her ass for the shit she was doing. Eventually she even started using coke and that shit was the last straw between us. I kicked her ass out and sent her on her way. At first she tried to get back with me and wouldn't' leave my ass alone. But after a few months it was like she fell off the face of the earth. That was almost two years ago.

Then she popped up out of nowhere a few weeks ago and fucked up my life. I wasn't exaggerating either. Everything had been going smooth between me and Shanice. I was so in love with that damn girl it wasn't even funny. I would do almost anything for her. The only thing I couldn't do was get out of the situation I was in now.

I couldn't deny my own flesh and blood. Angela came back with a little girl who she claimed was mine. She was over a year old and the math added up. I knew in my heart she was mine even before I got the DNA results back. She had the same smile as my mother and the test only confirmed what I already knew.

I was keeping this shit from Shanice and waiting for the right time to tell her. Now I was really fucked because the way she caught me over here made it ten times worse than what it was. Angela was trying to get some dick since coming back but I wasn't about to cheat on my woman with her ass. Shanice was definitely gonna think we had something going on and I couldn't blame her. That was if she even was willing to hear me out. I already knew she was gonna try and leave me for this shit without listening to shit I had to say. I would bet her ass was gone before I even got home.

I didn't know how I was gonna get myself out of this, but I wasn't trying to lose Shanice. I was gonna do everything in my power to make sure she stayed with my ass.

Messiah (Money)

Larissa was really pissing me the fuck off. I called her ass a few times back to back to see what the fuck she was up to. I wasn't with her leaving MJ with my mama all of the sudden like she did. When I came over here I was surprised as shit to see my son here instead of with LaLa where he was supposed to be. Even though me and Larissa wasn't fucking around or together I still knew her schedule for school and where my son was at all times.

She pulled this shit last minute which had me thinking she was on some shady shit. If she left him here to chase after some nigga we definitely was about to have a problem. Thinking about that shit had me mad as fuck.

My mama came outside where I was standing in the backyard trying to get ahold of Larissa. She patted me on the shoulder and waited for me to end the call, which went straight to voicemail anyway.

"Boy you need to calm down. She ain't doing nothing but helping Shanice with something. I was trying to stay out of what ya'll got going on but I'm gonna tell you this. You either need to leave her alone or be the man she needs and deserves." My mother said.

She really never got involved with my personal shit or business affairs so I knew she really cared about Larissa.

"We're good. It's nothing for you to worry about." I tried to ease her mind.

The last thing I wanted was her worrying about my shit when she already was stressed out over Emeri's ass.

"I'm serious Messiah. You need to get your stuff together!" She responded with a raised voice staring my ass down like I was a little ass boy again.

"Alright, I got you." I said while holding my hands up like I was surrendering.

My mama was no joke and I would never go against what she told my ass. I decided to take MJ home with me since I was done with my business for the day and already hit the block early to check on a few of the spots. I wasn't on the block hustling or anything. All I had to do was drive through the hood and that was enough to be seen by those niggas who stayed plotting.

Most of the work I put in these days was meetings to make sure shit ran accordingly. I still scheduled shipments and pickups. Having linked up with Emeri and then becoming the plug was a whole different level in the drug game. My days of hustling on the block were like a distant memory. My hands rarely got dirty and sometimes I missed that shit, but not enough to go backwards. I was bringing in millions of dollars a week and had plans on raking in more.

Lately I was thinking more about expanding our enterprise and opening up a few more businesses. I really didn't have a fucking choice since I needed more clean businesses to keep our shit looking legit and the law off my back. I did have some good ass investments going on too, but it wasn't enough.

I also started buying real estate in each of the states we were doing business. I closed several deals on different properties over the last couple months and now it was time to upgrade Larissa's shit. I wasn't about to have her or my son living in a fucking apartment no matter how nice it was while I had multimillion dollar homes all over. Once she finally figured out MJ was with me and not over at my mom's she would have to come get him. It would be the perfect opportunity for me to let her in on the plans I had. I already knew Larissa was gonna try and put up a fight about moving but I wasn't taking no for an answer period.

Me and MJ chilled out and watched TV before we both dozed off on the couch. His ass loved to act grown and run shit. He wouldn't let me turn away from cartoons without hollaring until he got his way. Just like his daddy he got what he wanted.

When I woke up MJ was still knocked out so I took him up to his room and laid him in his crib. MJ's room was as big as mine and it was filled with all the best shit. While I was upstairs I heard my alarm being disarmed. It was probably Larissa but I wasn't taking no chances.

I pulled out my pistol and walked down the stairs with it in hand. When I turned into the hallway leading to the front door LaLa was standing there and was startled when she heard me come up behind her. I slipped my gun into the back of my pants again and turned her around. I smelled the alcohol on her breath which let me know she had been drinking. That must have been some serious shit going on with Shanice because they usually only drank when they went out.

"Hey Messiah. I came to get MJ."

"The fuck you did! You ain't takin' him nowhere right now he's asleep and you been drinking." I said sounding meaner than I wanted to.

"Fine! I'll be back in the morning for him." Larissa snapped back at me, even rolling her eyes.

She should have known better than to cop and attitude with me.

"Come here." I said.

Larissa stood still like she was thinking about the shit instead of doing what the fuck I said. She was so hard headed but I loved her ass. My mama was right it was time to get my shit together and after tripping off the possibility of LaLa being with some nigga earlier I was ready to admit that shit. I was gonna try and bring our family back together and to work it out with her. I just hoped she was willing to give the shit another try. Fuck that she didn't really have a choice anyway.

"LaLa get your ass over here." I repeated.

This time she walked the few steps over to me so that her titties were touching my chest. I even felt them rise with each breath she took. I grabbed ahold of her shoulders and let my hands rest there while I leaned forward and whispered in her ear.

"Every inch is Mine Larissa." I said as I let my hands slowly traveled down her body squeezing her tits, kissing her neck and then finally cuffing her pussy through her leggings.

Her ass didn't say shit back but by her breathing I knew I was affecting her. I bet her pussy was leaking from that shit just like my dick was hard as hell right now. I pulled back away from her and walked past her into the living room. As much as I wanted to fuck I needed us to understand each other first. I had a lot of shit to run by her and wanted to do it all the right way.

LaLa walked into the room shortly after and sat down in the chair across from me. She slid off her shoes and tucked her feet in under her just like she always did when she got comfortable. It was little things like that which let me know how deep our love was. If it was any other woman I wouldn't have noticed none of the small things about them or how they acted. None of the other bitches I fucked around with mattered to me enough to pay attention.

I loved every fucking thing about Larissa and no matter how much shit happened between us or how much time we spent apart nothing would change that shit. Not even fucking other women or her being with another nigga. As much as that shit made me sick to think about, it wouldn't break what we had.

"So what's up Messiah?" Larissa asked straight up.

"I'm gonna keep it real with you. I want us to try shit again and be together. As time goes by my feelings and love for you don't do nothin' but get stronger ma. I know how bad I've fucked up with everything but me walking away was the only way I knew of protecting you. You would've never got shot in the first place if you wasn't with me."

"So let me ask you this, what makes you think you're gonna be able to protect me now? Or how do I know you're not just gonna leave again when shit gets tough? I been down this road not once but twice with you Messiah and even though I love you, I don't know if that's enough for us."

"I hear you shorty. But things are different now. I got shit on lock and I'm not the same small time hustler on the rise that I was. No mothafucka not even that nigga Torio is a threat. And any threats that will come up I got a whole band of niggas and security to handle that shit. I'm not letting nobody touch you or MJ. As for me leaving you. I never left you. Maybe physically, but you always have my heart and I'm gonna be there for you from here on out"

Larissa didn't say shit for a minute and when she did I was surprised as hell at what she shared.

"But Messiah it wasn't Torio that shot me, it was your ex Carina. It wasn't nothing to do with the street stuff you got going on. I love you Messiah but I just don't know about us being together."

"I'm not saying we pick up where we left off, but I want us to work towards that shit. You're gonna still be my wife one day and I bet my life on that shit."

"We'll see." Larissa said with some sarcasm in her voice.

She wasn't flat out saying no to my ass even after the shit I pulled leaving her when she was at her worst. So I was confident I could get her to open up to me again as long as I lived up to the shit I was telling her. I had one more thing I needed to let her know before I got in them guts.

"That's straight. But to start with I'm moving you and MJ to your new place tomorrow and I'm not taking no for an answer. I bought the house for us to live in together as a family but I'll wait to move in until you're ready to claim my ass again."

After laying everything out there we were both grinning at each other each other like some goofy ass kids. It was like we finally could be us again. I told Larissa to come over to where I was at and she stood up not waiting

126

to start coming up out of the clothes she was wearing. She knew what time it was.

She was butt ass naked by the time she made it over to the couch and immediately dropped down to her knees in front of me. She unbuckled my pants and pulled them and my boxers down so she had easy access to my dick. Her eyes always got big as hell when she looked at my shit. I loved how she enjoyed sucking my dick and the shit turned her on just as much as my ass. My size always intimidated her but she handled it like a champ.

"Do your thang ma. Swallow the monster." I said jokingly but serious at the same time.

Larissa started caressing my dick and showing it attention while letting spit drip down from her mouth making it extra sloppy before she deep throated it. Her eyes watered which let me know she hadn't been sucking any other nigga dick because she had to get used to it again. Once she let her jaws relax my baby went to work. She had my ass about to cum within minutes but before I got the chance she straddled me and let my dick stretch her wide.

Her pussy was tight as fuck and after about two strokes she was cumming. From then on I was the one taking charge and flipped her ass over. We fucked three times before morning and before I knew it the sun was shining in through my curtains waking me up.

LaLa wasn't in bed with me anymore. I got up and went into MJ's room where I saw her burping him in the chair. This was my fucking family and the sight of Larissa and my son being here with me was making me feel like a bitch for not making shit right sooner. I would die for these two and there wasn't no way in the world I was gonna walk away again. I would have to be six feet under first.

Larissa

Here I was back in Messiah's arms lying in bed with him. Was I one hundred percent sure I should be giving his ass another chance? Absolutely not. But we only had one life to live and almost losing my life after getting shot taught me to take more chances. I used to be so closed up to anyone and everything but the things that happened had changed me. I was still cautious but I was also able to admit when it was all said and done that I still loved Messiah. Despite how shit went down between us he was my other half. Being here with him feeling at complete peace confirmed it even more.

I was gonna take him up on his offer to move into the house he purchased for us, but I was also gonna wait to have him move in just like he suggested. We could be in a relationship but not jump right back in where we left off. We needed to take time to build the trust that was obviously lacking in our relationship previously.

Last night we made love and fucked back to back and my body was sore as hell but satisfied too. Since the last time after the Antoine incident I hadn't had sex and that seemed like forever ago. Which I wasn't even trying to think about at the moment. So I pushed that to the back of my mind and focused again on the conversation me and Messiah had last night.

I revealed to him that Carina was the one who shot me not someone connected to his drug shit. I read his expression and saw that he was surprised by what I told him. But I was still glad I let him know who was really behind it.

Messiah rolled over next to me but his ass was still sound asleep snoring and all. I chuckled quietly at him because he refused to ever admit he snored. I should record his ass then he couldn't deny it. I was up so there was no use trying to go back to sleep.

I went ahead and got up making sure not to disturb Messiah and went down the hall to MJ's room and of course his little butt was up and smiling at me. He was always so happy in the morning which melted my heart every single day. He truly was a blessing and made me want to go even harder and be better with everything I had going on.

I fed MJ and sat there burping his greedy ass when my man walked in looking just as sexy as I left him. He had on some grey sweats and no shirt. Even with his sexy dark skin I could still see the new tattoo he had across his chest with a picture of me and MJ. I didn't even know he got that done and it brought tears to my eyes. All this time I questioned his love and dedication to me but he was still keeping our love alive.

It was just a tattoo but that let me know the shit he was telling me last night was something he had put a lot of thought into and also let me know he was thinking about me just as much as I was thinking about him while we were apart. Messiah must have seen what caught my attention and of course had to make a comment about it.

"You like that shit huh?"

I nodded my head in response. I wasn't about to fill his cocky head up more. He already had enough of a damn ego. Once I finished burping MJ, Messiah went ahead and got him dressed and ready so I could shower and get dressed. He wanted to show us the house and planned on us moving in right away.

Messiah reassured me over and over on the drive over that things were different with his organization now and that everything changed since we were together before. He kept talking about all the properties he bought and how security would always be around so I didn't have to worry about anything.

I was just a regular ass woman who came from nothing. I wasn't ever with the material shit Messiah threw my way when we were together but I understood what he was really saying to me. He was trying to prepare me for being with him again.

When we were together a year ago he continuously stayed on me about how he needed me to be strong and hold him down. I had done everything he asked, even started to enjoy the lifestyle he provided. But what he was talking about now was something on a whole other level than before. I didn't know how I was gonna adjust to having security follow me around all the time, but Messiah told me that he had security on me all the time already. I was surprised as shit to hear about that because I never noticed being followed or watched. But it definitely sounded like something Messiah would do.

We pulled up to a property not too far from Messiah's other house. We turned onto a road I had never been on. It was more like a long ass dirt road which I learned was the driveway to the home. After about a mile the trees ended and we came to a clearing where there was a tall gate and security guard. When we stopped in front of it a guard spoke to Messiah and then looked at me smiling.

"It's nice to meet you Mrs. Lawson." He said politely.

I nodded in return, "You too."

Messiah said, "That's Jacob. He's the main guard. Anyone who comes onto the property has to show their ID and he'll run a check before they can enter the grounds." Explaining the security situation to me.

I listened and the thought of having 24 hours security did put me at ease. If what Messiah was telling me on the way was true I understood why he went to these lengths. It may have been a little over the top but at least I wouldn't have to be looking over my shoulder worrying about some shit Messiah had going on affecting me or MJ. He really wasn't exaggerating when he was telling me all about the way he had come up even more in the game because this shit had to cost a fortune.

Once we pulled through the gate the drive turned into pavement and led to a circular driveway. The house was more than I could have imagined. It was three stories and wasn't just a house, it was a big ass mansion. I knew Messiah was doing well but this was more than just good. The place was absolutely beautiful and I would be lying if I said I wasn't excited about this being our new home.

Before we got out of the car Messiah opened up the glove box and pulled out a deed to the house. He handed it to me and as I read through it I saw that I was the actual owner of the home not him. I was at a complete loss for words and leaned over and kissed him deep to show my appreciation.

Messiah led me on a tour of the home and then put in a few calls to have my things packed up and moved. He let me know the movers would be done by the end of the day. He really was that nigga who got what he wanted and made sure he took care of us. It seemed like things were looking up for me more than I thought possible. I was in college pursuing my dreams, had a healthy son and now the love of my life and me had reconciled.

I needed to get ahold of Shanice and make sure she was okay after that shit Silk pulled yesterday. Although I was happy as hell right now it didn't feel right knowing my best friend was hurting. I decided to call her up and have her come over so we could have some girl time. Hopefully it would be a good distraction for her and she could take her mind off of that stupid ass nigga.

I gave Shanice's name to the security guard Jacob like Messiah instructed me to do. He left a little while ago to meet up with his boys and discuss his plans on opening some new local businesses. He was definitely trying his hardest to gain my trust, making it a point to tell me where he was going and when he would be back without me having to ask. That was already better than how things were between us before. I hoped it lasted.

Shanice was still upset from the shit that went down yesterday and I couldn't do much to make her feel better. Silk really played her ass out and did her dirty. Especially how he told her to leave while he stayed to console that bitch he was fucking around with. I really thought he was better than that and would have never suspected he was fucking around on Shanice. Especially by the way he treated her. But I guess you could never be sure of anything.

When Shanice made it through the gate an alert went through on my phone from the app Messiah added earlier. There was various cameras around the property that had around the clock surveillance and when someone was on the premises it automatically focused on the car or person. I went ahead and closed the app making my way downstairs to the door. Which actually took me longer than would in a normal size house.

I was still getting used to the fact that this was all mine. Messiah giving it to me meant that no matter what happened between us, I would still have a place to live. It meant I wasn't dependent on him. He couldn't put my ass out, only I could kick him out.

"Hey Neesy! I'm so glad you came over."

I hugged Shanice like I hadn't seen her in year when she walked through the door. I didn't even wait for her to ring the doorbell before swinging it open to meet her.

"Awwwe you know I love your ass too bitch! Now this is a nice ass house. Messiah really doing it big huh? Your pussy still gold to that nigga I see!"

I appreciated the fact that Shanice was still able to be happy for me despite the shit she was going through. I wanted to take her mind off of things and knew she would fill me in on everything when she was ready.

"Yes girl, but this is all me. I got the deed and everything. We really gonna try this shit again and hopefully this time we'll get it right." I replied as I started walking down the hall leading Shanice on a tour of the house.

I couldn't remember all the different rooms but I would learn as I showed her. Once we made it upstairs to the master bedroom we sat down in the sitting area by the walk in closet and dressing room. It was my favorite place in the house besides the office and playroom. Messiah had really gone all out with decorating the house to suit my taste. The thought he put in that alone made me even more confident in my decision to move forward with our relationship.

"Messiah did a good ass job this time! I'm really happy for you girl." Shanice said.

"Yes he just needs to keep it up and not let me down this time. But how are you doing girl?" I asked referring to the blow up I witnessed yesterday.

"Fuck that nigga! He not only fucked me over but disrespected me worse than I ever been in my life. He did all that shit in front of that bitch too. I could kill both their asses!" She said all amped up.

But I could tell she was hurt behind the anger in her voice. I wanted to be real with her but also make her feel better as much as possible.

"I know you love his ass and I been through what you're going through. It's hard but I'm here for you."

"I know and I'm gonna be just fine. With or without a nigga I'm gonna be alright. Like I said fuck Silk's dog ass."

"Well I think we should go out tonight and have some fun. Let that man see that the shit he pulled ain't gonna keep you down.

Usually it's you trying to get me to go out, but this time I'm making your ass!" I teased.

"Okay bitch." She answered before slapping me high five.

Me and Shanice continued to chill out and relax the rest of the afternoon. I texted Messiah to let him know I needed to go out tonight with Shanice to help her take her mind off of things. He texted right back which surprised the hell out of me. He hadn't been that prompt in getting back up with me since he was first trying to run game on me when we met. I was really impressed, but it better last I hoped. He let me know that he would be home around midnight and would take care of MJ this one time as he said. Letting me know next time we would be going out together not separately.

We didn't even need to go out to the mall to get outfits since I had a full closet of fly shit still with the tag on them. All of the things Messiah bought me when I left the first time plus some new shit. It was like he just kept buying things for when I got back with his ass. It was sweet but also kind of fucked up since I was really planning on us being done for good.

Shanice was wearing a cream colored sheer dress with a built in bodysuit. She was looking more than sexy and would have every nigga drooling over her tonight. Her body was amazing and I swear her ass got even bigger since fucking around with Silk's ass. I decided to wear some cut off denim shorts and a simple black crop top. I threw on some knee high Jimmy Choo lace up pumps. We both kept our hair down. Mine was straightened and was just past my shoulders with some blond highlights. Shanice was rocking a few extra inches than usual so her hair was sitting just above her ass and was jet black.

We were headed to a spot downtown instead of the one on the north side I went to when I met Antoine. The last thing I wanted to do was cross paths with his ass. I still hadn't spoken to him since the day we had sex. There was no point in us having a conversation since there was absolutely no future for us. I would rather forget we ever messed around in the first place. Any feelings I had for him were better off being pushed to the back of my mind, especially now that me and Messiah were back together.

I chose to drive one of Messiah's new whips that was just sitting in the garage. He told me I could drive whatever I wanted, that everything that was his was mine so I planned to do just that. The cocaine white drop top Mercedes was calling to me since he first showed me it. I fell in love with it right away.

Shanice was damn near screaming when I showed her the cars in our garage. She was used to nice shit growing up the way she did. But the fact that Messiah upgraded my life the way he did she was just as excited as I was. That was another reason I loved her. She was never on that hating shit no matter what. Even when she could be salty because she was going through her own shit right now it just wasn't in her to be that way.

Once we pulled up to the curb in front of the club we saw that there wasn't a single parking spot anywhere near the entrance. I slowed the car down and that's when I got a call from Messiah. I answered it still looking around for a spot. We really didn't want to have to park in the parking deck and walk down to the club especially with the nice ass car we were driving.

"Hey baby." I answered.

"Sup sexy. You can stop where you at and get out. I got my niggas behind you and they gonna take care of the car while ya'll go in the club. They'll be out front when you're ready. Just hit me up when you 'bout to head out." Messiah said.

Him bossing up always turned me on. I loved when he took care of shit. I wasn't used to him keeping tabs on me like he was, but according to him he had been doing it for a long time. At least since he was back from Belize months ago.

I thanked him and made sure to agree to behave tonight before I ended the call. Just like Messiah told me to I stopped the car in front of the club and put it in park. Me and Shanice stepped out. Before we even made it onto the curb I looked back behind me to see some man I had never seen dressed in all black get into the car and drive off followed by a black suburban. I really had to get used to being with a boss ass nigga like Messiah.

This club was owned by one of Messiah's associates so they already knew who we were before we made it up to the line. We were ushered inside and led to a VIP section. A worker came over and took our drink orders. While we waited I pulled out a blunt from my purse. I used some matches in the section to light that shit up and me and Shanice sat back enjoying ourselves more and more as the effects of the weed hit us. I went ahead and stood up and started dancing once the new Meek Mill song came on.

Shanice was right there with me and we started to really turn the fuck up even more after we got our drinks. We told the server to keep them coming. We were on a mission to get fucked up tonight more than we usually did for the simple fact that Shanice needed to forget all about Silk' ass.

After about an hour I had to use the bathroom so me and Shanice walked down to where they were located. As we walked through the crowd it was hard to stay together because there was so many people in the place. Everybody was crowded together and there was hardly any room. I thought I caught a glimpse of that hoe Carina too near the stage talking to some nigga that looked familiar. When I looked back again to check and see if it really was her it was already too late and some other random people were in the place I thought I spotted her. I shrugged it off and figured if I saw her again it was meant to be.

Since the shooting I made sure to never leave home without my own heat. I had gotten a small nine and a license soon after my recovery. So if I had a chance I was more than ready to lay that bitch out. I was patiently waiting on my get back but best believe there wasn't any way I was letting her get away with what she did to me. Plus I knew she would come after my ass again if given the opportunity. So I wasn't gonna give her the chance plain and simple.

After using the restroom I pulled Shanice into the corner and told her about how I thought I saw Carina. I also let her know that I had my gun and planned on using it if I came in close enough contact with her. Shanice didn't even know Carina was the person who shot me until earlier today so she was more than ready to get at the bitch too. I had to pull her back from going towards where I saw her at. She may not understand but I really wasn't worried about seeing her either way. I was confident that when it was meant to be I would get my chance. I wasn't gonna force shit.

Finally we made it back up to the VIP section and to my surprise Antoine and a few of his niggas were posted up waiting for us in our section. He was bold as hell approaching me in public like he was and on Messiah's turf. I turned around to take my ass right back out of the area. I did not want to have a conversation with him and definitely did not want to be around his ass. It would be real disrespectful to Messiah too and I wasn't trying to fuck shit up between us before it even got started.

Before I had a chance to step down, Antoine grabbed my arm turning me around so that I was standing face to face with him.

"So it's true. You back with that nigga after everything. The least you could do was say the shit to my face shorty." Antoine called me on my shit without hesitation.

I did feel bad about how things ended up between us but there wasn't nothing to be done about it. I didn't know if Antoine knew Messiah was his brother or not or even if he was just using me to get at him. No matter what we had or could have had, it was better if we just forgot about each other altogether and moved on with our lives. There was no point rehashing old shit that would never matter anyway. I would never be with him knowing he was Messiah's brother.

"Yes, I'm with Money now. Is that what you want to hear? What we had is over. I'm sorry if I hurt you but I'm happy with him. So there's nothing more to say about it." I snapped back at him with more attitude than I intended.

It was bad enough I dropped his ass the way I did but there was no use leading him on whatsoever. All of the sudden Antoine's eyes turned cold and his gaze went to something behind me. Before I could look back and see what caught his attention I felt a pair of familiar arms wrap around me from behind.

Messiah clasped his hands together and pulled me back into his body which was rigid and tense probably because he was ready to flip the fuck out right now. I knew exactly how his ass was when it came to me. He had knocked a mothafucka out for talking to me before we really were even together. Now here I was standing and having a conversation with a nigga that I actually had been intimate with. The only other man in the world I had sex with besides Messiah. I was shaking because I was scared of what Messiah would do.

Instead of doing some crazy ass shit like I expected, Messiah continued to hold onto me and kissed my neck before whispering in my ear, "The way you bossed up on that bitch ass nigga got my dick hard La."

I instantly felt relieved and horny at the same time. Messiah must have heard the exchange between me and Antoine, and I was at least glad for that. But I was still feeling fucked up for how things ended between us. Antoine really wasn't nothing but good to me. It was something I would have to keep to myself because I didn't think Messiah would understand me feeling bad for another nigga.

Messiah returned his attention to Antoine who was standing in front of us with his gun drawn but down to his side. The gesture was threatening enough and Messiah's next words were directed at him.

"Homeboy you better take a look around before you make another fuckin' move."

Antoine looked around and noticed the various guards posted up near all sides of the VIP section with weapons pointed directly at him and his niggas. He saw that he was outnumbered and being that this wasn't his turf he was gonna have to hope he made it out of here without dying. I didn't want his death to be on my hands so I hoped like hell he didn't do nothing dumb. Antoine went ahead and dropped his gun to the ground and his boys followed suit.

"My wife's off limits nigga. You're lucky I'm letting you live this time. If you know what's good for you, you'll make sure I never lay eyes on your ass again." Messiah called out to Antoine as one of his security detail punched him in the face and grabbed his arms to drag his ass out of the section and the club.

Right as he was being pulled past us Antoine's stupid ass had the nerve to say some shit I was hoping he never mentioned again.

"Don't worry nigga, I already got a taste of the pussy and had her calling me daddy. You can have her nigga. She ain't worth the trouble." Antoine said before spitting blood out right onto Messiah and getting some on me in the process.

Messiah instantly pushed me to the side and started laying blows to Antoine's head and body back to back. Antoine wasn't even fighting back and I was scared that he was really dead by the time Messiah's guards finally pulled him off. It was like Messiah had lost all control and doing shit like this in front of the crowd that formed around wasn't good in case Antoine really didn't make it.

Once his guards told him they had it handled and that he needed to bounce Messiah grabbed my hand and rushed us out the back way of the club. Shanice was right behind us as and as soon as we got outside Silk pulled up fast as hell telling us to get in the car.

I knew the last nigga in the world Shanice wanted to be around right now was Silk's ass but we didn't have a choice since we already heard sirens headed our way. We rode in complete silence and I thought we were headed towards my new house until I realized we were going the opposite direction.

Silk gave Messiah some kind of note. His whole body language changed and he went crazy again. He began slamming his fists into the dashboard until Silk finally spoke up which seemed to calm him down a little.

"It's' already being handled bruh. I'll fill you in when we get to the warehouse. Trust me I got you." Silk said.

The rest of the ride was filled with an eerie quiet all the way to a building far from the city. I felt that something was really off but wasn't sure if it was just the shit that had happened back at the club, so I chose to wait until we got inside to ask Messiah about it. I didn't want to upset him more than he already was.

The building turned out to be some kind of warehouse that Messiah kept for business reasons. I had never seen or heard him speak about the place but wasn't surprised since it seemed like I was still learning more things I didn't know about his ass by the day. There was several cars outside the building like there was something going on but I found out Messiah kept a few extra cars here in case something came up. I guess this was something. I wanted him to explain what the hell was going, where MJ was and why we were all the way out here in the middle of nowhere.

Messiah (Money)

The shit that happened back at the fucking club was the least of my worries right now. When Silk handed that note to me my stomach dropped and I wanted nothing but to kill every mothafucka who had anything to do with the shit. The note was some kind of ransom bullshit for my son.

When I left out in the middle of the night to chase behind Larissa the last thing I expected was to be putting MJ in danger. I dropped him off while he was still sound asleep to my mama's house. The note not only left me wondering about how my son was doing but also what the fuck happened to my mother. I almost lost all control right away. But Silk promised he already had shit handled. I didn't want to go over all the details in the car because that would only cause Larissa to worry when I was doing enough of that for both of us. She was gonna completely lose it when she found out that MJ was taken.

We pulled up to the warehouse and I jumped out of the car fast as shit making my way inside. I needed to hear exactly what the fuck was going on and what Silk meant when he said it was already taken care of. I avoided LaLa by hurrying over to my office and Silk followed right behind. Draco was already inside sitting at the table but when he saw me he went ahead and followed Silk's ass too. Now all three of us were inside my office with the door locked. I would have to tend to LaLa afterwards, but for now I needed to get to the bottom of the situation. I wanted all the details first.

"What the fuck happened?" I asked getting straight to the point. There was no time to waste if my son's life was in danger.

"Some mothafucka's scooped up MJ from your ma's spot. They broke in and snatched him up. Your mama woke up to a noise but they was already gone with him."

"The fuck you mean? Where was the guards who I had outside?"

"They got hit. All of them were found dead sitting in the ride. Your mama is safe at your house right now. When she couldn't get ahold of you she called me and I took care of it. I know you had that tracking device put in Junior's chain so I told the security team pull that shit up. They got the location on him right away and we got a team surrounding the place until we pull up. They got eyes on him too and he's still asleep right now, see." Silk filled me in on everything as he handed his phone over which displayed a live video feed of MJ.

I felt a little better being able to see him and know he was straight. I was glad I went ahead and followed my gut about getting tracking devices installed in all kinds of shit MJ and Larissa wore. I wasn't taking no chances when it came to their safety.

"Alright let's ride out and get the mothafuckas. I'm not sitting around waiting while he's still with them niggas. Ain't no telling what they're capable of."

"There's more. It was Torio bruh and turns out that bitch Carina played a part in that shit too." Silk added.

I wasn't surprised it was either of them to be honest. Since Larissa let me know it was Carina who shot her I planned on offing her ass anyway. Now she was a dead woman walking. Both their asses were as far as I was concerned.

I hurried up and made my way back through the building. I didn't have time to go through everything with LaLa and decided it was best if I wait until after MJ was back safe and sound to let her know about the situation at all. She rushed over to me before I made it out the door and tried grabbing on my arm to get me to stop, but I just kept going. I shrugged off her hold on me and kept moving forward. She was yelling at me and asking me what was going on, I didn't want her to know MJ was taken. It would only make things worse for her. Finally I closed the door to the warehouse. Even though it was hard leaving her knowing she was worried she would understand later when I brought MJ back.

What was usually an hour drive back to the city we cut down to thirty minutes driving over a hundred most of the way. Luckily it was well past the time the clubs and bars closed so the police wasn't out like they would have been otherwise. Silk and Draco gave me directions of where to go based on the information the security was giving them.

We pulled into some old abandoned looking houses on the North Side near the projects. I was familiar with the area but never would have thought some niggas would be bold enough to try some shit like this against me and in my own city.

I wasn't about to sit around and wait while they played with my son's life either so once I pulled up to the curb and parked all three of us hopped out the ride. I wasn't scared to die but I would be damned if Torio did some fuck shit to my son. I walked up to the front door and kicked the shit in. Draco went around the back of the house and I heard him kick the shit in like I did. Silk was right behind me with his heat pulled ready to murder some mothafuckas.

Torio's dumb ass really thought he was gonna kidnap my son and he wouldn't be touched. The nigga was sitting on the couch with some stripper bitch riding his dick. He was doing all this with my fucking son in the same house. He must have been the stupidest nigga alive.

I walked up to the bitch and let off two in her dome. She was guilty by association. I guess that got Torio's attention because he opened his eyes and tried to jump up dick swinging and all. I didn't have time to play with his ass either like I would have if MJ wasn't here. Tonight he was lucky and would get a quick death even though he didn't deserve that shit.

I used the rest of the rounds in my glock to lay his ass out too. I wanted to make sure his ass was dead. That was a mistake a lot of niggas made but I wasn't one of them. When I killed a mothafucka he stayed dead. I walked through the house to where I heard MJ crying. Draco and Silk checked the rest of the house and made sure the shit was clear.

It was too bad Carina's ass wasn't here. It was only a matter of time before I caught up with her ass too. Her days were numbered and before I got back to the warehouse and told Larissa I would make sure every nigga in the city and fuckin' state was looking for her ass.

I picked MJ up and he instantly calmed down. The feeling of having him safe in my arms was the best feeling in the world. If something would have happened to him I would have lost my mind for real. He was a little G though and came out untouched even with the bullshit going on around him.

When we turned back onto the drive leading to the warehouse I instructed Silk and Draco not to say anything and that I wanted to explain everything to LaLa myself. Draco just sat in silence while Silk agreed. His ass was still acting funny about the shit that went down when I was in Belize. But fuck it I wasn't gonna worry about his ass. If he wanted to act like a bitch that was his problem.

As soon as I opened the door Larissa ran over to me and quickly took MJ out of my arms. I guess it was her motherly instinct that was telling her something was really up because she was holding him close and kissing him all over just like I had been doing when I found him.

"My baby is safe and sound." She cooed to him before sitting down in one of the chairs at our big ass oak table.

She could have sat down in the game area where we had couches and been more comfortable. By her choosing to sit at the table instead told me she wasn't ready to relax and I didn't blame her. I sat down at the head of the table next to where she was sitting, in the seat I usually sat in when I discussed business with Silk and Draco.

We still hadn't expanded to the point we let any other nigga know about this spot even though the table sat twelve. Maybe one day we would let a few other trustworthy niggas in on our shit. But what wasn't broke don't need to be fixed.

Once Larissa felt MJ was settled enough asleep in her lap she looked over at me and I realized she had been crying. Her eyes were bright red and puffy. I felt like shit knowing I left her here to worry without saying shit. But getting to MJ as fast as I could was more important than her feelings at the time. I expected to catch hell for it now though.

Larissa continued to make eye contact as she spoke.

"Tell me everything Messiah. What happened to my baby?"

I told her everything I was told including the parts where I found out that fuck nigga Antoine was spotted at the club. How I decided to come up there to make sure he didn't try no funny shit, all the way to how I handled Torio's ass and found MJ.

"Thank you. I don't know what I would do if anything happened to him." She said while she placed a hand on my shoulder.

"You know I got ya'll. I'm not letting nothing or nobody fuck with you and I'm gonna make sure no other mothafucka touch one of ya'll again. That's fucking with me now, but I'm gonna fix that shit. You got my word." I told her.

I was definitely gonna take care of Carina and step up the way I did shit even more. I wouldn't make the same mistake again. It was time I moved my mama up out the hood too like I had been trying to get her to do. I already bought her a house down the road from our home. I was gonna stay true to my word and be the boss nigga my family needed me to be.

Now it was time to take my family home and put this shit behind us. Even though my uncle was still on the run, by taking care of Torio's bitch ass I cut off his legs. I was confident that his ass would be dead soon and I wasn't gonna sit back this time. Tomorrow I would start making moves. After saying our goodbyes to my niggas and Shanice we were back on our way.

Once inside I went with Larissa to settle MJ in. It was five o'clock in the morning so his schedule was gonna be all fucked up. I figured his ass would be asleep for a couple more hours which was fine because I had shit to do and didn't plan on sleeping the day away when there was money to make. I needed some pussy before I would be able to sleep especially after all the shit that happened. I needed to feel that shit.

LaLa still had on those little ass shorts she wore out to the club and was still looking good as fuck. She began to undress taking off her heels first. I walked up behind her and slid my hand up under her shorts sticking my fingers in her pussy. Of course she was wet as fuck right away. After playing in it for a minute with her leaned up against the bed bent over. I went and unbuttoned her shorts pulling them down rough as hell.

Larissa put her knees on the bed and tooted her fat ass up in my face. I dove in head first eating her pussy from the back. I was flicking my tongued hard over her clit and then stuck it as far as I could in her pussy. She started trying to scoot up further on the bed to get away from me but I wasn't having that shit. I wanted her ass to stay still so I could really fuck up her head. So I reached up and started playing with her titties from underneath. I squeezed her nipples and then cupped them both so she couldn't get away from me and run from my tongue game.

She screamed out before her body started shaking and her cum gushed out and I licked that shit up. After her climax her body was weak and she just about collapsed on the bed. I knew her ass was tired but she hadn't even taken the dick yet. So with her laying there I placed my two hands on her ass and gripped the hell out of it as I watched my dick slide into her pussy.

Sometimes I went easy on her ass, but this wasn't one of those times. I wanted her to forget all about that nigga Antoine and ever fucking with him. Even though I played that shit off back at the club what he said was still fucking with me. I didn't want to think about another nigga feeling what was only meant for me. And I damn sure didn't want Larissa to ever think about fucking another nigga. Once all eleven inches were inside her. I stayed planted and started rotating my hips.

"Messiah I can't take it! Shit I can't!" LaLa screamed at me.

She was really serious too, but the way her pussy was soaking wet told me something else. I wasn't letting up on her one bit.

I pulled her back further by the hips and continued moving in a circular motion causing LaLa to cum back to back. Her body was shaking and still I kept going.

"Take the dick LaLa. It's my pussy right?" I asked even though I already knew the answer. I wanted to hear her say that shit.

"Yessss daddy, fuck me. Fuck your pussy." LaLa got up enough energy to start moving with me. Her pussy was clenching down on my shit too.

I wanted to see her pretty pussy so I stopped and turned her around. I lifted her up and laid her down in the middle of our big ass king size bed. I spread her legs as wide as they would go almost into a split since she was flexible as fuck. I grabbed her ass from underneath and lifted her up so her pussy was positioned right at the height of my dick.

I entered her again and with us both watching that shit this time, before I let go of all control and started really fucking her. She had her hands pushing up against the headboard so that she was fucking me back. Her titties were bouncing up and down with each stroke I took and we were staring into each other's eyes.

"You bet not ever give my pussy away again. We in in this shit for life."

I looked down at LaLa and gave her an intense ass look to let her know even though we were fucking I was dead ass serious. If she fucked another nigga I just might kill her ass. I wasn't sharing her or her pussy with no other mothafucka.

"Yes Messiah. I'm all yours." She said giving me the same intense look back.

Once she said that shit I released a big ass nut with her cumming on my dick at the same time. I stayed with my dick inside her afterwards for a minute and repeated the same thing I said while we were fucking.

"Larissa I'm dead ass. This my pussy and I ain't sharing so don't do that shit again. You're mine". I said before kissing her.

"Same to you then. I'm not sharing. That's my dick." She replied while clenching her pussy muscles to let me know she wasn't fucking around either.

We laughed and then I rolled off her. We both fell asleep after that satisfied and comfortable as fuck. It felt good to have my family safe and sound and for us to be together again. Shit was really working out even with niggas plotting.

Shanice

For some reason shit was just not working in my favor right now. Here I was trying my best to stay away from Silk's ass only for me to have to not only be near him because of the shit that had gone down with MJ, but I was in the same fucking car. Not to mention, now it was just me and him so there was no other distraction like I had earlier when we were all at the warehouse.

In there I was able to avoid him even when he tried to pull me to the side. There wasn't any way I could get out of hearing what he had to say now. So I was preparing myself for it before anything even came out of his damn mouth. Right now I hated his ass and everything about him. So I wasn't gonna really be listening to anything he had to say anyway. Fuck him!

"I'm sorry for that shit yesterday." Silk finally got enough nerve to say.

We were already riding for a while before he came out with it. I wasn't about to go along with the shit. I was determined to keep my mouth shut. There was not a fucking thing I wanted to say to his ass or hear. We were done and that's all there was to it. A few more minutes passed before he realized I wasn't gonna say shit to his ass.

"Listen Shanice it's not what you think. I never cheated on you and that woman wasn't some bitch I was fuckin'. She's my baby mom. I just found this shit out. I got a shorty and I was trying to figure out a way to tell you. The last thing I wanted was for you to find out some shit like this the way you did."

This mothafucka really expected me to have some kind of reaction. But when I said fuck him and I was done I meant it. So what if he decided to come clean about the shit after the fact. It was too late. I wasn't about to believe anything coming out of his mouth since he wasn't up front about shit from the jump. So I didn't believe that he wasn't fucking around either.

But even if he didn't fuck the bitch he still played my ass yesterday. He didn't stand up for me and I was supposed to be his woman. He chose that bitch and his child over me. I understood that it was his kid but I didn't sign up for that shit. At least he could have given me a chance to know what the fuck was going on instead of letting me make a fool of myself the way he did. As his woman I should have been the first person he came to when he found out.

But it was obvious he was a coward and he didn't love me enough to be honest about it. So I sat there in silence and continued to think "Fuck that nigga". He wasn't worth a fucking reaction, just like I wasn't worth confiding in. What we had was done the moment he failed to keep shit real with me.

We were nearing the house that we shared together up until yesterday. I moved in with his ass and we had been staying together basically our whole relationship. I didn't have another place to go, but I already thought it over and planned on staying at a hotel for a week or two. Then I would find something more permanent. Money was never an issue for me since my parents were always more than generous. My accounts were full even before Silk gave me the stacks to spend. I deposited most of that shit too.

"I'm staying at the Marriott downtown," I finally said.

Those were the only words I said to him and even though it wasn't what he wanted to hear that was all he was gonna get out of me. He must have realized I wasn't budging and didn't try saying shit else either. A few minutes later he pulled into the hotel parking lot and stopped in front of the entrance. I opened my door and was planning on leaving without so much as a thank you.

"I love you Shanice. Remember that shit." Silk said before I closed the door behind me.

I continue on my way not looking back once. After booking my room for a few weeks and checking in I was finally alone in my room. I was able to let out all the tears I had been holding in the whole time I was around Silk.

I swore I wasn't gonna let him see me cry since I did enough of that yesterday. But now, here alone in my room I was able to break down. Silk really hurt me and I was broken hearted. He didn't trust me or love me the way I did him and I couldn't be with someone who didn't value me the way he showed me he didn't' by keeping shit from me. It was better if I said goodbye and moved on without him in my life because the way I was feeling I never wanted to feel again. I really loved that nigga.

Larissa

It was the end of October and for the time being everything seemed to be working out for the best in my life. Although getting back with Messiah started out tumultuous with MJ's kidnapping the last few months were completely drama free for us.

Messiah stayed true to his word and made sure we were one hundred percent safe and I was comfortable with the security he provided for our family. Ms. Sheila was living closer to us and that made things a lot easier as far as watching MJ. Especially with the crazy ass class schedule I kept. I decided working part time would be too much and take away from the time I had to spend with MJ who was growing so fast as it was. He would be a year old in three months and I was starting to plan his first birthday party.

He was the happiest little boy alive and brought so much joy into all of our lives. I was truly beyond blessed to have him. I finished both summer sessions of classes with all A's and B's and was now into my first full semester of college life. My goal was to finish my degree in three years instead of the typical five.

Being a mother did nothing to slow me down, it actually had the opposite impact on me. I wanted to grind even harder for him. I would never be a woman that depended on her man no matter how much money Messiah gave me or spent on us. I just wasn't cut out that way. There was nothing like being able to hold your own. I appreciated what Messiah did for me and MJ. I was finally able to fully accept the way he spoiled me where it was hard to when we first got together.

Today Shanice and I planned to meet up and get our nails done so that we could finally spend some time together. It had been a couple weeks since we got an opportunity to be around each other. Although we saw each other on campus and had a class together, we didn't get to just hang out. I was busy at home and she was busy staying busy. Since her and Silk's breakup she had been wildin' out.

Shanice wasn't hoeing around but she did decide to join a sorority and was fully engaged in college life and everything that came with it. So even though we were around each other most of our free time was spent doing different shit. I wasn't stressing it too much because I knew it was her way of coping with the break up and it wouldn't last forever.

I knew she took the breakup hard. It also didn't help that Messiah was Silk's best friend and some of the places and events we went to he was at too. I knew with time she and I would be spending more time together so I had been laying back letting her do her thing. Today was the first time we were actually going to do something one on one outside of school in months so I was excited as hell.

I made it to the nail salon earlier than our appointment and everything. Shanice was a few minutes late like usual which made me laugh when she finally did come in the door.

"There's my bitch!" She said while I stood to give her a hug.

"I should have known your ass was gonna be late." I jokingly said back.

Shanice and I went ahead back to the technicians doing our nails. We were getting manicures and pedicures so we decided to have a glass of wine while our feet were soaking and we were sitting in the massage chairs. I really loved getting my feet done more than anything because the massage chairs and wine.

"So what's new with you best friend?" I asked once we were relaxed.

"Just chilling girl. Enjoying life and making the most of the college thing. I still have a week to decide if I'm gonna pledge the sorority. You know I'm not with taking orders and shit. And before you ask I'm gonna tell you straight up I'm not fucking with any nigga." She said the last part in a dramatic way making sure to put emphasis on the word fucking.

Shanice always said what was on her mind and she knew my ass was about to grill her about that shit.

"I'm glad for you girl. Live your life! To keep shit real, Silk is seeing someone new."

I had to keep it real with her after all she was my friend not him. If my ex was moving on I would want to know. Her expression got real tight and it looked like she had lost her best friend before she responded.

"Good. It's better that way." She told me before closing her eyes and leaning back in the chair.

I wasn't done though I really wanted her to know that I understood and was here for her. I could tell she wasn't as over Silk as she was trying to act.

"I'm just gonna say this once. I know you love that man Neesy. I know it's hard. I been there girl. I think ya'll need to talk."

"I appreciate you caring LaLa, but I'm good."

After she said that I left it alone. I figured if they were meant to be they would work it out just like me and Messiah were doing. Silk pulled me aside a few times since their breakup to ask about Shanice and how she was doing. I avoided his questions and always told him that she was doing fine.

The new bitch he was seeing he brought around a couple times and I couldn't stand her ass. Not only because she was my best friends replacement but because she seemed like a gold digger and was always asking too many damn questions. She gave me a bad feeling, so much that I even brought it up to Messiah but he shrugged it off telling me not to worry about shit that didn't concern me. He trusted Silk and wasn't worried about any "bitch he was fucking" as he told me. I would definitely be keeping an eye on her though.

After getting our nails done we decided to go out and grab some dinner before we parted ways. Since we both drove separate Shanice was going to follow me to the restaurant so we could leave from there. I really wanted to go to the hibachi spot and get some of their good ass food. We were driving down 3rd street when the car in front of me slammed on their brakes and I didn't have enough time to stop before my car slammed into the back of them.

My head whipped forward and hit the steering wheel but other than that I was fine. My car probably was a little fucked up but nothing too major. I got out planning on going to see about the person I had rear ended when the security team following me intervened. They pulled me back and went ahead to talk to the other driver. Shanice also got out of her car and came over to where I was standing.

I thought the security team was overdoing it but apparently they were following Messiah's orders so I couldn't be mad. He was just trying to keep me safe. When one of the men saw my forehead was bleeding he insisted I be taken to the hospital and told me Messiah would meet me there. Shanice agreed to drive me there even though I thought it was just a waste of time, there was no use arguing with everyone. I decided to go along with it.

The emergency room was actually pretty empty which was unusual because it seemed like the place stayed packed. I was able to be seen within fifteen minutes and sitting in the back. They went ahead and took a urine sample and basic blood test to make sure my kidneys hadn't been affected by the seatbelt during the crash. After doing a physical and letting me know there was no more external damage other than the contusion to my forehead they gave me some Tylenol. I was left waiting for the rest of the results which I knew would come back fine as well.

I was already feeling better by the time Messiah was let back to the room that I was in. He left MJ with his mother which made me feel relieved since the hospital was the last place I wanted him to see me at even if it wasn't something serious. Messiah came over to me and gave me a big ass hug squeezing tight. He always acted like I was so fragile when I really wasn't.

"Why you always gotta scare a nigga?" He asked trying to sound serious.

"I'm fine really. I wish you didn't make me come here as it is. I hate hospitals." I complained sticking out my bottom lip pouting and everything.

"I'll make that shit up to you when we get home. The monster gonna make it all better."

He said grabbing his dick which made my mouth and pussy water.

I swear this man was the sexiest man alive and he was serious when he said monster dick. It always made me feel better even if I felt like I was gonna die while taking it. The doctor came in and both of our attention went to the older white lady who had a smile on her face.

"Congratulations are in order Ms. Bradshaw. Otherwise you have a clean bill of health and you will be out of here shortly." The doctor announced happily.

I was completely caught off guard at what she was implying so I blurted out, "Excuse me? Congratulations?" I questioned her.

"Yes miss you are just over four months pregnant. The baby is perfectly fine. I would suggest you follow up with your OBGYN in the morning and I wish you the best. It was a pleasure." She said reaching her hand out for me to shake.

I shook her hand still in shock. I had absolutely no idea I was pregnant all this time. I didn't have any of the symptoms I did when I was pregnant with MJ. No morning sickness, moodiness or being tired as hell all the time. I really was feeling great this whole time and here I was already into my second trimester. I was also taking birth control faithfully so I definitely needed to make sure that wasn't gonna harm the baby. My mind was racing trying to take everything in and the next thought I had was what if it was Antoine's?

This was the very first time I thought about his ass since the club encounter. But I needed to be realistic about the situation. I had sex with him around the time if my math was correct and we didn't use protection. Although I wanted it to be Messiah's there was a chance it wasn't.

Me and Messiah were having sex more than once a day but according to how far along the doctor said I was I had to have gotten pregnant the time he came over after the weekend in the mountains. I was already too far along to consider an abortion not that I would anyway. MJ was still young but there wasn't any way I would get rid of a baby after making it work with my first born. I was confident enough in my mothering abilities and in my drive to still complete school.

When the doctor left Messiah came right up to me and the crazy look that his eyes let me know he was thinking about the same shit I was. He knew that I fucked Antoine and him around that time. He was a smart man so I was sure he put two and two together.

"We'll talk about this shit when we get home." He said in a cold voice.

I nodded my head and led the way out down the corridor towards the exit of the hospital. I was really starting to get in my feelings about the way Messiah was acting. Even though he hadn't said anything yet I knew him well enough to be able to know exactly what he was gonna say. He wasn't happy about me being pregnant. I understood he didn't want me to have a baby by another man, but I still wanted him to be supportive no matter what. We weren't together at the time. If it had been under different circumstances and he was sure the baby was his and no one else's he would be ecstatic about the shit. He always talked about how he wanted to keep my ass pregnant and have a houseful of kids.

I needed him to understand that no matter what the baby growing inside me was still part of me. Plus I felt that the baby was his too, even though we would have to wait until I gave birth to find out. I knew all about getting a special amniocentesis but I wasn't gonna risk that shit harming the baby.

Once we made it to the house I hurried the hell on out of the car and slammed the door to the house behind me. I was mad because Messiah's ass hadn't said shit on the ride home either and here I was pregnant and going through just finding out too. It wasn't like I planned this shit.

"You can kill all that fuckin' attitude you got LaLa." Messiah yelled when he stepped inside.

But I wasn't trying to hear what he was saying. I wanted his comfort and for him to tell me everything was gonna be okay. I needed him to be my rock because I was worried just like him. I didn't want to have a child with someone other than him.

"Whatever. Are we gonna talk about this?" I wanted to see where his head was really at.

"I need time to think on the shit first. I know it might be that nigga's and I'm not 'bout to be raising another nigga seed. If you hadn't opened your fuckin' legs this shit would of never happened." Messiah said.

"Damn it's like that nigga?" I shouted at his ass.

It was one thing for him to be honest, but he was being more than disrespectful. He was really ready to say fuck me yet again. I just didn't understand how a person can be all about loyalty and claim they love your ass but every time shit gets tough they're ready to bounce. That's what Messiah always did to my ass and I wasn't gonna go through this shit for the rest of my pregnancy. I was not about to be worrying whether he was gonna leave me or not over something that I couldn't even control. It wasn't like I could go back in time and fix my mistake, which really wasn't a mistake.

At the time I wanted to have sex with Antoine. We had been dating and were in a damn relationship. Messiah made it seem like I was hoeing around but that wasn't the case at all. Maybe that was what was fucking with him too. He knew I had feelings for a man besides him. I didn't know, but whatever he was going through with coming to terms with me being pregnant I still needed him to make a decision. Either he was gonna ride it out with me for better or worse or we could go our separate ways yet again.

The baby growing inside me was completely innocent to all of this and I would never subject my child to being treated less than. This was also an opportunity for Messiah to show me if his love for me was real or not.

"I don't know Larissa. The fuck you want me to say? I'm a real ass nigga and I'm trying to be honest. That's what you wanted right?" Messiah responded to my question.

"What the fuck ever. You either in this shit with me or you not! That's what I want to know." I told him with a calmer tone. I needed an answer.

"And I'm telling you I don't know. I need time to think about this shit." He held firm to what he said in the beginning of the conversation.

I turned around and walked my ass upstairs stomping my feet and everything. I was mad as hell. I wasn't trying to be over the top but he was pissing me the fuck off. I wished he would come upstairs behind me and wrap his arms around me telling me he loved me and wouldn't leave me. I really wanted his comfort but he did the opposite. He turned around and left back out the front door, got in his car and drove off.

I laid down and let the tears flow. It had been a long time since Messiah made me cry but here I was going through it again. This time it wasn't all on him though. I was part to blame and I knew that shit deep down. I was the one who laid down with another nigga and that was one thing Messiah was right about. No matter how many bitches he fucked I wasn't dealing with a baby mama out there or some bitch claiming she was pregnant. At least not since that Carina shit that happened before me.

I didn't know if it was fair of me to expect more from Messiah. Maybe he was right to feel the way he did, but it still hurt either way. Finally, I said a prayer asking for God to make things right in our household and then finally drifted off to sleep.

Messiah (Money)

I didn't know what the fuck I was gonna do but I really couldn't see me raising another nigga seed especially my own fuckin' brothers. Shit was so fucked up and the best thing for me to do was put some distance between me and Larissa. I wasn't trying to leave her ass either.

This time I was gonna stay by her side and see if the baby was mine or not before doing shit I would regret. Maybe I should be a better man and tell her shit was gonna be okay and I would step up no matter what, but I wasn't that nigga. I would be lying if I let her believe some shit that wasn't true. So instead of getting into a fight over shit that couldn't be changed I decided it was best to just leave and get my mind off things for a while.

I had the important business meeting coming up with the families in New York and Miami coming together. This would be the first time I proposed the shit I had in mind and it could change the way our enterprise operated from here on out. If the deal went through it would mean even bigger shit than we were already experiencing. I wanted to bring one of the biggest bosses from New York into my organization and another young boss from Miami.

I was already supplying the nigga in Miami but the deal I was proposing would elevate him to the head nigga in charge of the whole state of Florida and the boss from New York would be much the same. By aligning our interests I would be the supplier of the entire East Coast with the product coming through Belize.

I wanted to allow these niggas to come into Money Makers Inc. and really run shit. It was a big ass opportunity for each of them but after watching how they conducted business I really felt like it was the right move for our organization.

I still had to deal with my father and find Fe's ass but I already was moving in on that nigga Fe. He was up in New York which worked perfect since I was heading up there for the meeting. I was gonna take care of both issues with one trip.

In the meantime, I was opening up a new strip club in town. I lived for this legit shit too. It amazed me that I was just as happy running the legal businesses as the street shit. There was something about investing money back into my hometown that would never get old to me. I wanted to eventually open up more businesses across the country, but keeping it local was important to me more than anything else. I loved my city and would always keep a level head about shit. I wasn't one of those niggas who was gonna forget where I came from or not look out for my niggas and people

I've known my whole damn life. I just wasn't that type of nigga.

After that shit with LaLa I drove over to the building that was being turned into my club. It was on the Westside of town more towards the college which was good because it meant the police were gonna be kept out of my shit for the most part. The building was almost finished and the contractor was completing the last touches on the inside. I had a general manager that was in charge of all the staffing and expenses but at the end of the day the shit had my name on it so I was always gonna make sure shit was running right.

I was in my office going over the final budget and was happy as hell because we actually were coming in under budget. Whenever it meant more money I was all about that shit.

There was a knock at the door and my nigga Joe opened it a crack to tell me there was some bitch looking for me. I told him to let her in and wasn't thinking too much of it until Chyna's ass came strutting in with a smile on her face. I had to admit she was still fine as ever and to my surprise she wasn't dressed in the stripper shit I usually saw her in. It had been a minute since I saw her ass. The last time I saw her was when the Larissa caught us fucking. Just thinking about that shit got me heated like it just happened even though it was like a year ago.

"Hey Money." Chyna said as she sat down.

"Cut the shit Chyna. The fuck you want?" I asked.

Her being here wasn't a good look for me. If LaLa showed up, even if it was unlikely, my ass would be in deep shit and I wasn't trying to get caught up behind some bitch I wasn't even fuckin' with like that.

"Damn, it's like that? You don't miss me, not even a little bit daddy?" Chyna really asked me like what we had was something more than fucking.

I laughed and said, "Nah, I'm good over here. I got the best pussy waiting at home shorty." I grabbed my dick out of habit and caught her looking at my shit like she was ready to hop on it.

She was thirsty as fuck but her pussy was good. Not anywhere near as good as my lady's though. Those were the only walls I wanted to feel now or in the future. After staring at my dick for a minute her look of desire was replaced with one of disappointment before she continued with what I guess she came here for.

"Well anyway I was wondering if you could look out for me and hook me up with a job. I won't cause no problems between you and that bi.... Your woman." Chyna wisely corrected herself as she asked for a job.

"I tell you what. Tomorrow I'll bring my wife with me and if you still want the job you can ask her for that shit. If she say yes then you're on, if she say no, then that's that."

Any decision I made that came this close to home I was gonna let LaLa be involved with. Plus I figured it was good to keep shit on the up and up between us. It would also give LaLa a chance to really handle Chyna however she saw fit. I was gonna start letting her be more involved in my business. It was only right since I wanted her to be my wife and we already had a family together.

With the thought of our family my entire mood shifted back again to LaLa being pregnant. I realized there wasn't no way I was leaving her ass. The only way we weren't gonna be together if we was six feet under. I meant that shit. I was gonna make shit right with her and be supportive through everything. That nigga Antoine was already a dead nigga walking so if the baby she was carrying was his it wouldn't matter anyway. I was that baby's father and I wasn't gonna accept anything different.

Coming to that realization I started to get up and leave so I could make it home to my baby. Her ass was probably stressed the fuck out with the way I left out. Even though it was so late, I wanted to make shit right ASAP.

I passed Chyna's ass still sitting in the chair across my desk without a word. I guess she could tell I wasn't saying shit else on the issue. She was either gonna show up tomorrow or not, I didn't give a fuck one way or the other. I didn't owe her shit.

Once I made it home I walked inside and noticed all the lights off. MJ was still at my mother's house since LaLa had the accident earlier. We were gonna pick him up in the morning from down the road.

Inside our bedroom LaLa was sound asleep and her ass looked comfortable as hell. But I wanted to wake her ass up and make shit right. After the shit that went down in Miami when I left before speaking to her I never wanted to leave things fucked up between us. You never know when your time is up or you won't get the chance to talk to the ones you love again. I learned a lot since all that shit went down. I was trying to be a better man all the way around. More people were counting on me and I didn't want to let them down.

I leaned down and started placing kissing on LaLa's shoulder. She opened her eyes and smiled up at me. Even though I left when we were on bad terms, the fact that she was able to wake up smiling no matter what said more about the type of person she was. Honestly she was more than a down ass rider, she was what niggas only dreamed about finding and she stuck by me through all the bullshit I put her through.

I intentionally let my hand fall lower where it was covering her stomach. I wanted her to know I meant the shit that I was about to say.

"This is all me. I'm in this shit for life LaLa."

"But what about..." She began before I cut her off with a kiss.

"Ain't shit else to say. No worries ma I got you, we good."

I didn't want to discuss it anymore. She didn't need to be worried about a damn thing. It was my job to take care of her and make sure her and my kids was straight period. I would take care of the fuck nigga anyway.

Larissa went ahead and let the shit go like I wanted. She was fully awake now and sat up in bed waiting. She knew I wanted to get inside that pussy. So she started tugging at my pants unbuckling them first. My big ass dick sprang out right in her face. I grabbed the back of her head pulling her hair out of her face and holding it back so she had full access to the monster.

LaLa used her tongue and licked my entire length from the balls to the tip before she began sucking on the top half of my dick. She was really working her jaws and then all of the sudden let the rest of my shit slide down her throat. I started fucking her mouth while I kept my eyes trained on her and she did the same. I was so into it that I didn't let up when she started gagging a little but she didn't seem to mind. The head she was giving just got sloppier from her spit and I finally tensed up and let my nut go. She sucked and slurped until I was completely drained.

I pulled the covers all the way back and off the bed. I didn't want shit to get in the way of the fucking we were doing. I moved forward and pulled Larissa's shirt up but not all the way off. I like the way her titties were bunched up from it and I squeezed each one pinching her nipples before sucking on them using my tongue to circle them and biting down teasing her even more.

"I want the dick Messiah." Larissa begged me between moans.

"You want it, Come sit on that shit shorty." I said while sitting down on the edge of the bed.

I was serious too, if she wanted it like she said I was gonna let her take it. I didn't give up control easily. But whatever she wanted she got.

"Yes daddy, I'm gonna take it all." She said talking dirty while she got fully undressed and then hopped off the bed.

She stood in front of me naked smiling down at me. She looked like she had some shit in mind to do and I was more than ready for whatever the fuck she wanted. I was in her hands right now. Larissa went to the bedside table and turned on some music. Then she started dancing to the shit giving me a lap dance. She was really putting in work like she was on stage or some shit. My baby was doing her thing.

LaLa lifted her leg onto the bed so her pussy was near my face and started rotating her hips to the beat. Then she turned around and bent over in front of me. She started making her ass bounce to the beat. I slapped that shit leaving marks. That made her go harder with her hands planted on the ground. I couldn't help but appreciate her sexy ass body that was all mine, so I slapped her ass a few more times and reached in my wallet pulling out the stack I had in there. I let the hundreds rain down on her completely naked body. That really made her ass go wild and she placed both her feet on either side of me while in a handstand. Her pussy was right in my face while she was letting her ass do its thing.

After the bills were scattered all around her I went ahead and slid two fingers in her pussy. She continued making her shit twerk but now she was moving to the rhythm of my hand. I wanted to make her cum and see that shit close up. So I kept going and finally just like I knew her ass would, she started shaking and then her cum soaked my fingers. I leaned forward and used my tongue to clean the rest of it up before lifting her up and bringing her down on my dick without warning. She screamed out from the way my dick busted her open. I needed to feel her after that shit she just did.

LaLa put her hands on my knees for support and started riding my dick reverse style while I leaned back on my forearms so I could grip her ass and spread her wider while she worked my ass over. She was screaming out and finally her whole body stopped moving which let me know she was about to cum again. Instead of letting her stop I held her hips and started fucking her from underneath until we both cummed again.

"Damn I love your dick." Larissa confessed and we both laughed.

"Don't forget that shit either shorty." I said right back to her ass.

The truth was I loved her pussy probably more. I didn't care either that my ass was whipped. There wasn't nowhere I would rather be than laid up in her pussy.

We woke up early the next morning and I filled Larissa in on everything going on with the businesses including the legal and illegal shit. I wanted her to step up and learn more of the ropes so if anything happened to me she would be straight. I didn't want her to get caught up in the street shit but her not knowing nothing at all was also a big risk and could be a liability for her if some shit did go down. I wanted to make sure she was set for life with or without me.

I would do anything for her or my kids and they were my main reason for grinding so hard now. It was more than just making money and stacking that shit to satisfy my hunger for it. I wanted to stack that shit for my family now and leave a legacy behind to be remembered by. Like I said, I had grown up a lot over the past year and my whole outlook was different than it was when I first met LaLa. I knew that she was the reason I had changed for the better.

We were gonna go to the new strip joint then head over to Money Makers Inc. headquarters downtown so I could go over all the paperwork with her. It would take her a while to learn everything but Larissa was smart as hell and so I didn't have a doubt in my mind she could figure shit out in less time than most people.

I told her about the meeting in New York that was coming up and told her she was coming with me. The other niggas I was meeting with were gonna bring their spouses too. I wanted to build our enterprise with mothafuckas that had families like me. That way they would be more invested in the shit we had going on.

LaLa had grown a lot too since we got together. She was definitely on her grown woman shit and went hard for the ones she loved. She was exactly the woman a boss nigga like me needed. She was level headed, someone I could trust and loyal to the end. Not to mention beautiful as fuck and her pussy was the fuckin' best.

It really seemed like we were coming into a whole other level that we were meant for. I was happier than I had ever been and I felt my time as a real kingpin was approaching. This week was gonna set a while new beginning in motion for us. I was ready to have my family set for life and generations to come.

Carina

I couldn't' believe those mothafuckas kept fucking with my life more and more. I was back staying at my mama's house. Back exactly where the fuck I started all because Money and his bitch wanted to live happily ever while taking everything from me. First he got with that hoe, then took the DNA test and now he killed the one nigga who loved me in the whole world.

What was worse is that I didn't get shit out of any of it. I was still broke and still having to fuck niggas and trick off their asses. I didn't want this life and now instead of just worrying about me and my sister I had a whole fucking child to worry about on top of it. My life was really fucked up right now and every single day that I lived in this house I kept thinking of a million ways I was gonna get my revenge on Money and that bitch.

Then the other day I got an unexpected phone call from Torio's father. He was on the run but once he heard about Torio being killed he wanted to make some moves to take down Money. He asked if I would meet up with him because he already had a plan in mind. So tomorrow I was meeting with him in New York. I was gonna leave Monae with my sister. It was better if she kept her anyway since I had too much shit going on to be raising her right now.

For the first time since Torio's death I had something to look forward to. I couldn't wait until Money and that hoe Larissa got what they deserved. I was gonna do everything in my power to take their asses down. That bitch would be wishing she never laid on eyes on my nigga to begin with.

Larissa

Messiah letting me learn more about his business and other shit he had going on was like us moving to another level in our relationship. This was the stuff he never talked about or let me in on. I knew he did that to protect me, but with him telling me he was really showing me that he had grown and was looking at more long term things. I was honored that he not only loved me enough to share this part of his life with me but also a little intimidated.

I didn't want to let him down or fuck something up. He wasn't giving me control of anything yet, but he hinted at the fact that he would be including me in decisions he made. He reassured me that he trusted me more than any other mothafucka alive so he was sure I could do it. I just wish I had more confidence in myself.

Messiah kept talking about our future and our family's future legacy. I had never heard him talk like that before and although it was amazing to see the change in him, it made me wonder if there was some reason for this sudden change of heart. I decided to take Shanice's advice from the when I first met Messiah and just go with it. That was kind of my motto ever since that day and so far I hadn't been led wrong. Even though we went through our shit, I really wouldn't give up what we had for anything.

We were going over the finishing details for the strip club and Messiah was explaining everything to me when that bitch who I caught fucking my nigga came into the office. She had the nerve to sit down and smile at me like nothing ever happened between the two. I looked over at Messiah's ass immediately and he shrugged his shoulders before saying,

"She came by asking for a job yesterday. I told the bitch my wife made the decisions so she could ask you."

I smiled back over at Messiah. He really was being up front with me. I appreciated him for that shit, but the fact was the hoe across from me fucked my man and I saw the shit with my own eyes. I was glad he gave me the opportunity to come face to face with this bitch. It felt like I finally was gonna have a chance to move forward with a clean slate from what I went through in the past with him. After seeing her today I knew I would never have to worry about her ass again.

I turned and smiled in the stripper bitches face next before asking, "What's your name again?"

She replied sweetly with, "I go by Chyna, but you can call me Chy."

This bitch really thought shit was good between us. I slid my hand inside my purse and pulled out my gun. I wasn't about to play with this bitch. I stood up and walked around the desk right up to the Chyna bitch and pressed the barrel to her forehead. She looked up in shock and I felt her body trembling under the weapon. Messiah wanted me to boss up and be the woman he needed.

I was a woman who wasn't gonna put up with his infidelities or disrespect. The fact that this dumb bitch thought it was okay to come here and speak to my man in the first place let me know she didn't get it. She should have never shown her face then I wouldn't be holding my piece to her head. I turned and looked over my shoulder at Messiah who of course had a smirk on his face with a crazy ass look in his eyes. I knew he had to be surprised, but shit this is how he made me.

I turned back towards Chyna and pulled the trigger. Her head pretty much exploded and I backed up dropping the gun on the floor. I wasn't sad that I took her life, but I was still in shock with the fact I actually did it. I never thought one way or the other about killing so I didn't know how I should feel. It was like a weight was lifted off of me but I also was a person who believed in karma and the thought of how this would come back on me crossed my mind. Messiah made a phone call and then grabbed my gun before putting it in his pants pocket. He wrapped his arms around me.

"I got you ma. I know why you did that shit. Don't sweat it. I love your ass LaLa. Got my dick hard as fuck."

Hearing Messiah's voice and reassurance instantly made me feel better about my decision. I still knew I would pay somehow for taking a life. That was just the way of the world, but that was the world we lived in. I was a part of Messiah's life and we were connected so there was no escaping killing for me. Being with him taught me it's either kill or be killed. I was really in this shit now and there was no turning back.

I knew what my actions meant. They meant so much more than offing some bitch I caught him fucking with. I was in some way accepting a new lifestyle. I did what needed to be done so we could move forward.

I didn't say anything back I just gave him a kiss before we both left out and a couple niggas Messiah had working for him came in the office. It was a good thing the place wasn't opened yet and no one was able to hear the gunshot besides people who worked for Messiah, or should I say worked for us.

Messiah (Money)

I never wanted this life for Larissa but for us to make it I realized from early on that she was gonna have to become a small part of it. I wish I could keep her from experiencing the shit that came with me being in the streets, but that wasn't fair to her or my kids. I needed her to be strong and be able to hold shit down. Not just for me but for them. I was a nigga with a target on my back at all times and so was she. Whether it was jealous ass bitches or niggas plotting on us we would never be able to relax a hundred percent unless I was out of the game completely and that wasn't an option at this point. Maybe one day I could let it all go, but I doubted that shit would ever happen. The streets were in my blood and hustling was a part of who I was.

Larissa killing that bitch Chyna was something she decided to do on her own. I really didn't think shit was gonna go that way. I didn't even know she was carrying a gun like that. Sure I had seen her little heat but knew it was something more for protection than anything else after her shooting. I couldn't lie though seeing her boss the fuck up and do that shit turned me on. I was a sick mothafucka and never claimed I wasn't. I loved hard as hell and sometimes I liked to kill. Only God could judge me.

We just arrived in New York and the meeting was set up for tomorrow night. I wanted to get into town early enough to make sure everything was set up accordingly. I didn't want no bullshit to go down. The last time I had a scheduled sit down was with Fe, when he was still my connect and that shit left a bad taste in my mouth. I never wanted to be backed into a corner like that nigga did in Miami.

Me, Silk and Draco were all here and planned on going out to dinner with ladies before we went over the plans for the meeting again afterwards. We were staying at the Hilton and all rented out suites in the upper levels. Our rooms were next to each other's and I wanted to make sure we had a good ass time tonight giving everyone a chance to enjoy the success we were feeling. I never let my guard down all the way but having my niggas and Larissa by my side had me feeling fucking invincible.

MJ didn't come on this trip with us just in case something happened during the meeting tomorrow. I didn't' want him anywhere near here. He was staying with my mother again and it was really the first time LaLa had been away from him for more than a couple nights since he was born so she was a little on edge. But I knew shit would be good with the security I left watching over him.

We were planning on going to some Japanese spot in the city a block away from the hotel, but were still gonna ride over. I arranged for us to have a few whips and they were all top line shit. It was nothing but the best for me and my team.

When Larissa came out of the closet wearing some shit that showed off her body I was instantly ready to fuck. I knew she wasn't gonna go for it since we were running late so I let her ass go but not before I gripped her thigh and used my other hand to check and see if she had on any panties under her dress. She was always trying to be slick and walk around with her pussy out like I wouldn't kill a nigga over her ass. She had me crazy as fuck behind her ass. She had been a good girl this time and actually had some shit on.

I slid them mothafuckas to the side and stuck my finger right in her pussy. She squeezed her muscles trying to play like she wasn't loving my touch. Her juices were coating my finger already so I pulled my hand away and licked her juices off.

"You are so nasty Messiah, you ain't doing nothing though." She playfully said as she slapped me on the arm.

I grabbed a hold of her hand and brought that shit down on my dick to let her know I was more than ready to put her ass in check. She knew when it came to putting this dick on her I was not playing and would make her ass scream my name and have her walking with a limp if she doubted me.

"Okay I'll handle that later. I promise."

She got the message loud and clear. I kissed her on the cheek before scooting her in front of me and letting her lead the way out. I wanted to watch that ass as she walked. I loved everything about Larissa from her feet to her ass and smile. She was all mine. She was almost four months pregnant and now that I knew that her ass did seem fatter and her hips were filling out. I loved that shit even more because it meant more to grab onto while I was hitting it from the back.

When we arrived at the restaurant it was like the whole street shut the fuck down. Our whips were all foreign and drew attention not to mention we all looked like money. Me and my niggas were young and wealthy so wherever we went we demanded attention and respect. Inside the restaurant we had a special room designated for us and this was actually the first time we were all gonna be out with our ladies together. We were still waiting on Draco's slow ass to arrive. That nigga was always late and we were all used to that shit.

Finally he decided to grace us with his presence and my mood instantly changed when I saw the bitch he had on his arm. I would have never thought in a million years my nigga, my own fucking cousin would be fuckin' with my old fling. The same bitch who

I was fucking with back in Belize was now here in New York with my damn cousin.

I instantly reached for my pistol but kept that shit under the table so nobody saw it. I wasn't trying to pull the shit out here but I would if I needed to. There was no way that Che wasn't on some shady shit. I didn't know what was up with Draco's ass but he better not be on no fuck shit. The whole fucking situation wasn't sitting right with me. I had a feeling Che had some kind of ulterior motive.

The two of them sat down. Draco and Silk started talking and the whole time LaLa's eyes were trained on me. She must have known some shit was up by my expression. My baby knew me inside and out and could tell when something was off. I wanted to pull her to the side and explain who Che was but before I got the chance the bitch beat me to it.

"It's nice to meet you, I'm Che." She had the nerve to speak to my fucking wife and hold out her hand for her to shake and everything.

Larissa replied with a dry hello. I could tell she wasn't feeling the vibe Che was giving off and I couldn't' blame her. Then Che turned to my ass and smiled big as hell.

"Hey daddy. We missed you!" She said while rubbing her stomach.

The dress she was wearing had concealed her bulge, but now that she was sitting down I saw some shit I wished I didn't. Che was clearly pregnant and from her greeting she was trying to pin the baby on my ass.

I pulled my pistol out and pointed it right at the bitch's face. I didn't care who the fuck she was pregnant by. She came her to fuck with my old lady and knowing she was hurting LaLa meant I was ready to kill her ass right here. I turned my attention next towards Draco's ass with my heat still pointed at Che.

"The fuck you doing Draco? You my nigga, my fuckin' cousin and you bring this bitch to our dinner?" I asked.

He knew my ass was crazy and cousin or not his betrayal would get him killed regardless. I was ready to kill my own father and brother so he should have known better.

"Damn it's not that serious Money. You got LaLa so why you worried about who I'm fucking?"

Was this nigga serious? He was really trying to act like he didn't know the bitch was here on some bullshit. I was on ten and would end up catching two bodies right in this room. So instead of getting into some shit with Draco's ass I focused on the most important thing. I grabbed ahold of Larissa's hand and noticed the tears streaming down her face. She hadn't said anything but I knew she was hurt behind the shit.

I got up and walked towards Draco and before he knew what was coming I threw a punch to his temple knocking him off balance.

He didn't get a chance to come back at me since Silk grabbed him before he could jump. I grabbed onto Che's arm and looked her straight in the eyes.

She must have realized what my ice cold stare meant because her fucking smile she had been wearing instantly disappeared. While I was holding her arm getting ready to tell LaLa not to listen to the bitch she got up and made an exit out of the room with Shanice following right behind her.

"Baby or not I don't give a fuck. You better stay the fuck away from me and my wife or it's lights out."

I left out of the restaurant. LaLa was already gone so Silk came to my ride holding Draco by the arm. He didn't have to drag his ass out like I would have thought since he proved to be a damn snake. It made me wonder if he knew how bad he really fucked up.

I planned on getting to the bottom of whatever the fuck he was on. I had always been able to trust Draco but since I came back from Belize he kept acting funny as fuck then he pulled this shit. I would have never thought my day one nigga would betray me, but at this point I wouldn't put shit past his ass.

Shanice

Things were getting so much better for me since deciding not to pledge the sorority. It turned out the same bitch Silk called himself fucking with was one of the Soros and that alone let me know that shit wasn't meant for me. I was glad about how shit worked out though because she happened to bring his ass to one of the barbecues off campus that I was also attending. Needless to say from that day on I had my man back.

She was mad as fuck and tried to act like she was gonna do something about it but she knew better than trying shit with me. When me and Silk laid eyes on each other it was like we instantly were drawn to each other, just like we always were. I wasn't angry with him anymore since Larissa filled me in on the full situation. It took me some time but I realized that all he was doing was trying to protect me from being hurt.

He hadn't fucked around on me or done what a lot of other niggas did. He fucked up with not telling me some important shit that he should have done the first night he found out about it. So I was still upset but not to the point I wouldn't get over it. I felt like me and Silk were meant for each other. The time we spent living together was filled with nothing but good memories. We didn't fight and argue like other couples. We talked so many times about our future and made plans to one day marry each other. I was completely in love with that nigga and some small bump in the road wasn't about to change that shit.

When he asked me to come to New York with him I was happy for the getaway especially since I knew my best bitch was going. We would get to hang out plus I would have alone time with Silk. It was a win-win.

Now here I was looking at that bitch Draco brought and was ready to put hands on her ass. After Larissa walked out the restaurant I followed right behind her. She was upset about that bitch saying she was carrying Money's baby and I didn't want her to be alone. Since we didn't have the keys to none of the rides, we started walking back in the direction of our hotel. It wasn't that far anyway.

"I know he wasn't cheating or nothing but damn I don't want my man to have a baby with that bitch." Larissa let me know.

"It probably ain't his anyway girl. That bitch look shady as hell so don't worry about that shit. Money's ass ain't going nowhere."

"True, but it still hurts to think about him having a baby by someone else. I guess that's how he felt about our situation." She replied.

"What are you talkin' about? Did you forget to tell me something?" I asked.

I really wanted to to know, because it sounded like she was going through the shit now.

"I'm pregnant again. But it might be Antoine's." Larissa answered quietly.

"Damn. How did Money take that shit?"

"He said it's his no matter what. So I got no right to be feeling the way I do and being hurt by some shit that happened when we obviously wasn't together."

"Fuck that. Feel however you want. Ya'll will get through this because you two are meant for each other. And I can't believe your ass kept that shit from me. I wonder if my new niece is gonna favor Money or Antoines fine ass!" I said jokingly to lighten her mood.

"Whatever!" Larissa laughed.

No matter what I was confident that Larissa and Money would get past whatever came their way. They had been through some shit and still found a way back to each other. We made it back to the hotel in no time and Larissa said she was tired and gonna take a bath to relax. I gave her a hug and reassured her that shit would work out for the best. We each went into our hotel suites and I instantly kicked off my heels. After the walk back my feet were killing me.

I was ready for Silk's ass to get back. He already had me horny as hell during dinner rubbing on my leg under the table and saying nasty shit in my ear. I sat down on the couch and turned on the tv while I waited. A little while later he came through the door but my thoughts of fucking went out the window. He had Draco's stupid ass with him.

It was an awkward silence. Neither one of them were saying shit and I wasn't about to get my ass involved in the fuck shit Draco had going on. I didn't think there was any excuse for bringing that bitch on this trip or dinner with us. He should have known better and if he didn't he was stupid as shit. I guess Draco realized how bad he fucked up and decided to get everything out in the open because he started talking. It wasn't my business so I started to get up and walk away when Silk reached out and wrapped his arm around me from where he was sitting in the chair. He pulled me down on to his lap and whispered in my ear.

"Stay your ass right her girl. I don't wanna murder this nigga so it's better that way." I could tell he was being serious too so I stayed my ass put.

I didn't want him to get locked up for killing Draco's ass plus that was still his boy after all. If there was some kind of acceptable explanation he had for bringing that bitch he might not deserve to die.

"Bruh you know I'm not on no fuck shit. Ya'll my niggas. I didn't think bringing the bitch would matter. Money was done with her ass and me and him shared bitches before." Draco said explaining himself with a shrug.

He really didn't get it. I was glad that Silk spoke up because I wanted to knock his ass out for how stupid he was being.

"Nigga that bitch just tried to say that baby was Money's and play his ass. Your loyalty should always be to your fuckin' brothers. That bitch's whole reason for coming with your ass tonight was to pull some shady shit. You should have known better." Silk held up his hand to stop Draco from defending himself and finished with, "And you trying to tell me you didn't know none of this shit?"

Draco looked defeated. I read his facial expression and knew he didn't know all that shit Silk was speaking on but it didn't change the facts. He should have run that shit by his boys first and then he would have known. There wasn't no excuse he could come up with to make that shit right. He had fucked up for real.

All he said was, "I didn't know man." in a low voice.

Silk was done with the conversation and I knew the shit Draco pulled was fuckin' with him just like it was fucking with Money. They were all they had in the game and loyalty was the most important shit in the streets. Draco broke the trust between the three of them and I had a feeling that nothing would be the same for any of them from here on out.

We were in the bedroom and Silk looked stressed the fuck out. I wanted to relieve his stress so I stripped down while he was laying across the bed with his eyes trained on my body. I was gonna make him feel better like he always did for me when something was wrong.

I slowly made my way over to him on the bed and straddled his legs just below his dick. I didn't want him to do much work so I undid his pants with him lifting up enough so I could slide them down enough to release his dick.

I put my hands firmly on his chest and even though his shirt was still on his hard muscles underneath were well defined. I loved my man. He was built like the boss ass nigga he was. I lifted my body up and then let his dick slide all the way in my pussy. My muscles tightened up right away causing my body to shake while I let out my first cum. I was wet as fuck now so I started really putting it on his ass.

Silk wasn't one to let me do all the work so he began digging in my guts deeper and faster while gripping my breasts hard as hell. I screamed out in pain and because he was hitting all the right places. I swear his dick was like magic. He always hit all the spots that I didn't even know existed.

"Shit Silk, it's too big."

"Stop that baby shit and handle it like a big girl." He replied with a slap on my ass.

His words turned me on even more so like he said I started really riding his dick even harder. Planting my feet on the bed and working my ass each time I came down. I leaned down and kissed him while he was gripping my ass cheeks and squeezing them. He used his grip on my ass to move me up and down while I was still cumming before he tensed up and his nut filled me up. I laid there on top of him for a few minutes still kissing on him.

He was so damn sexy and I loved him more than I ever loved any other man or ever would. I really knew at that moment that we were going to be together for life. It may have sounded corny but he was the only one for me and I knew that shit without a doubt.

Larissa

I didn't know anything about the bitch Draco brought to dinner tonight. But from the moment she walked in I noticed an instant change in my man. Messiah's whole demeanor went from being in a good ass mood to looking like he was gonna kill somebody. That's when I knew some shit was up.

Then for her to claim to be pregnant by him was something I wasn't expecting. Messiah always claimed to use condoms with every woman besides me. But the first time I caught his ass fuckin' around he wasn't strapped up and now this Che bitch claims to be pregnant. He was really reckless with his dick. I left the restaurant because thinking about him fathering a child outside our relationship was hurtful.

I knew that me being pregnant and the possibility of it not being Messiah's made me seem like a hypocrite but it still hurt. When I got back to the hotel I wanted to take a bath and get my thoughts together. I was gonna stick it out with Messiah because he was doing the same for me. I had no choice but to deal with the shit. If that was his baby I would have to play the step-mother role. The alternative was for me to walk away from Messiah and I wasn't gonna do that.

I really believed in fate. So her coming with Draco tonight was a good thing in my eyes. From Messiah's reaction I understood he was fucked up behind Draco's actions. They were boys and more like brothers. He trusted him to have his back out in the streets one hundred percent so him doing some shit like this seemed like betrayal. I really had more faith in Draco than that. He may have been dumb as hell, but I believed he didn't know about the shit that bitch pulled tonight. He wouldn't break that trust between them if he knew. I wasn't about to speak on it to Messiah though because I knew him well enough to know that he wouldn't hear shit I said until he calmed down and was ready to hear reason.

After getting out of the bath, I oiled up my body and admired my reflection in the mirror. I was starting to show just a little and as I rubbed the oil over my stomach I came to a peace about everything. I was pregnant with a child who might not be Messiah's and he didn't hold it against me so I would do the exact same for him. I loved that man and was not gonna let anything or anyone come between us. I went out to the balcony where I saw Messiah sitting.

He was smoking a blunt and looked to be in deep thought. I sat in the chair beside him and placed a call back home to check on our baby. Ms. Sheila face timed me so both me and Messiah were able to say goodnight to MJ before he went to sleep. She reassured me that he was behaving and she was fine handling him for a few days. She told me to enjoy myself. I ended the call and then went over to sit on Messiah's lap with nothing but my robe on.

Messiah was leaned back smoking a blunt so I knew he had a lot on him mind. I wanted to talk about the situation and let him know I was gonna be by his side no matter what. But instead of talking I decided to show him. His dick was hard and the moment I put my hand on it he put the blunt down and undid my robe. We fucked on the balcony in Miami so it was only right he fuck me on one in New York.

The next morning I woke up completely naked in the big ass bed we had in our suite. When I reached out Messiah was already gone. I then rubbed on my stomach like I did every morning since learning I was pregnant. I didn't like being pregnant much but it was worth it to know my baby was growing inside me. I was more than grateful that Messiah had stepped up and decided to be with me and a father to the baby no matter what the results were. I felt like the baby was his honestly but couldn't be certain of anything until the DNA test.

I decided I was going to do the amniocentesis without letting Messiah know and then share the results once they came in. I didn't want him talking me out of it. It was something I wanted to do for us. I felt like we could really be at peace once we knew. I scheduled the appointment for next week and planned on having Shanice go with me for support. She was a little skeptical of the procedure but would always support me no matter what.

I stretched and sat up before I remembered that Shanice and I had plans to shop before heading to the meeting with our men. I was nervous and excited about the first real meeting I would be a part of. I hoped I represented Messiah well and didn't let him down.

After getting ready and saying our goodbyes, me and Messiah headed our separate ways with plans to meet back up this afternoon at the hotel. Today was gonna be a great day for us as a couple and for Money Makers Inc.

Messiah (Money)

I was in a tight spot with the shit that went down all because of Draco. Right now I was thinking murder when it came to that nigga. Even after a night to sleep on the shit it was still rubbing me the wrong way. He had been acting funny as fuck and now that shit with Che was the damn icing on the cake. How the fuck was I supposed to put my trust in a nigga who seemed to be going against me. I didn't know what the fuck had gotten into him but his decision making was all fucked up.

Silk filled me in on what he said last night when confronted about the situation. He was trying to act like he didn't know what he did was fucked up. Even if he didn't know about the shit that Che pulled about being pregnant, he did know I fucked her. He should have never thought it was cool to bring the bitch around my wife. To top that shit off it wasn't like we were back home and he was just fuckin' around with the bitch. He actually brought her up here while we were on an important ass business trip. That had to be the dumbest shit he could have ever done.

I was really questioning whether Draco should even be on the team anymore. If I couldn't' trust him then there was absolutely no way we could work together. I didn't want him involved in the meeting this afternoon and sent Silk to let his ass know. For now he was out and that was all there as to it. He could feel however the fuck he wanted about it but I had to look out for everybody's best interest and at the very least his head was fucked up right now. I didn't have time to be worried about that nigga. This was bigger than his ass.

I set this meeting up so that the East Coast would be on lock and under my control. I was proposing a good ass deal to these bosses this afternoon but if the slightest thing went wrong it could fuck my whole plan up. A lot of mothafuckas would die if shit went left so I was gonna make sure that shit didn't happen. Plus this was the first time we requested the women to be involved in shit. So it was extra sensitive.

LaLa and Shanice went out to the mall earlier and wanted to get some new shit. Those two could always run up a check together but I didn't sweat that. I wanted my baby to have everything she wanted and more. She was nervous but I was confident that she would help seal the deal this afternoon. I wanted to make the men feel secure and see the bigger picture behind our deal. I needed this deal to happen. It would allow me to start taking steps towards cutting my father out as the connect.

I was gonna be able to step up and replace that nigga as the head of the cartel. If this new alliance was formed, the amount of weight we were gonna be able to handle would triple.

Plus with the addition of these bosses and their organizations to my own team would make a good ass argument for the families under my father and Mexican cartels to let me step in my dad's spot.

I still planned on taking his ass out but I wanted to take over with as little interruption as possible to our money flow. If I got Emeri's men to turn on him first there wouldn't be resistance from the real powerful mothafuckas who backed his ass. Then I would only have to take him and a few of his loyal niggas out and shit would run smooth. Our organization alone had me on the fucking top. With a few other big time names added to what I already had going on there was gonna be no stopping me. That was why the meeting was so important. It was really gonna push Money Makers Inc. to the next level and I was ready for that shit.

We were meeting with a nigga who was the king of New York. He ran a tight ship and hadn't expanded past the state border but had shit on lock from what I saw. I learned all about the nigga first from my brother Biz. But to make sure he checked out, I sent a team up here to study how he conducted business over the last two months.

He never showed a weakness and was smart as hell. I linked up with him a few weeks back and had been in contact with him since. I didn't get into too much detail over the phone but let him know I had a proposal for him that would be low risk and high reward. He was more than interested and wanted to set that shit up ASAP. He apparently knew exactly who the fuck I was already and had heard nothing but good shit. I wasn't surprised that my name was ringing bells in the streets. Since becoming the plug and returning from Belize my drugs were flooding the streets.

The other man was an associate I already dealt with down in Florida. He was based out of Miami and proved to be a loyal and hardworking nigga on my team already. He wasn't officially on my payroll but I was his supplier and he was as official as they came. I was confident about the two niggas I chose to fuck with and build with even further. I just hoped nothing fucked up happened at the meeting.

The last time I had a meeting out of state like this was when Fe and Torio's bitch asses set me up. That led to me being taken and held captive in Belize. That shit may have worked out for my benefit in the end, but I wasn't about to go through nothing like that again. That's also why I chose where we were meeting and had the place filled with my team already. Nobody was gonna be able to out man me or out gun me this time. I wasn't taking no chances period.

Larissa never returned back to our hotel from her shopping spree with Shanice. So I went over to their room and started banging on the door. I was mad as fuck because she wasn't answering my phone calls either. I knew she was still upset about the shit that happened last night with Che, but I thought we were on good terms at least. She never brought anything up to me about it and it seemed like she was gonna stick it out with me. Silk answered the door with Shanice right behind him. They both were dressed and ready to go to the meeting.

"What's up Money?" Silk asked.

"I'm looking for LaLa. She didn't come back from shopping with your girl." I told him.

Shanice spoke up and said, "We got back an hour ago and she stayed downstairs to handle something at the front desk. She told me to go ahead upstairs without her."

I was really starting to think some shit happened to her. It wasn't like her to pull some shit like leaving. I turned around and got my phone out to call my security. I had them all at the building where the meeting was being held. Usually I would have kept some niggas tailing Larissa but I pulled them earlier so they could make sure the spot was secure. If anything happened to her I was gonna lose my damn mind. Just as my head of security answered I received a text message from Larissa.

The message said, "Money I left. I can't be with you and put up with your shit anymore."

I didn't know what the fuck Larissa was on, but I made it clear to her ass that there wasn't no breaking up. I instructed two of my security teams to leave their post and track her down. Her cell phone and purse had tracking devices in them. I would deal with her after the meeting. I knew the thought of Che having my baby was fucking with her, but what we had was bigger than any of the bullshit that came our way.

The meeting went exactly as I planned. I let everybody at the table introduce themselves including the wives of the other bosses. I wanted to emphasize family and how with us making this deal it was bigger than just being the boss of our city or state. I was the only one who didn't have my wife by my side. That wasn't sitting right with me. I was counting on Larissa and she let me down with this shit. Maybe she wasn't as ready as I thought she was for this life.

Each of the other niggas also brought their right hands and when it was all said and done we had created something bigger and better than any organization out there or that came before us. We even talked about making plans to expand West with more members on our team as time went on. I liked the idea but I was always more of a keep shit small and see how it goes first type of nigga. I didn't want to get ahead of myself but in the future there was no telling. In time loyalties would be tested and we would see how shit played out.

Larissa

I was down in the hotel lobby asking the concierge to take care of the surprise I had for Messiah. He had a lot on his plate right now and then to add to that Draco and Che pulled that shit last night. My man was really dealing with a lot of shit. I was upset last night, but after getting myself together I was gonna stay by my man's side through it all. I was gonna surprise him with a nice dinner for two on our hotel balcony. I wanted everything perfect. It was gonna be similar to the dinner Messiah had set up for us in Miami with candles and everything. I wanted to put his mind at ease and also celebrate the deal I was sure that he was gonna make at the meeting later.

After settling everything with the concierge I turned around to pick up my shopping bags and was surprised as hell to see some man holding them already. He was tall and dark with eyes similar to Messiah's.

"These must be yours." He said in a deep accent.

My guard immediately went up. The man was obviously here for a reason and I could tell he knew exactly who I was.

"Let's not play games. Who are you and what do you want?" I asked the man with an attitude.

I didn't have time to waste entertaining this man who had something up his sleeve. He smiled back at me with an evil ass grin before setting my bags back down. He pulled out his cellphone and handed it to me. I saw a video of Ms. Sheila and my son. In the video there was a masked man holding them hostage. Messiah's mother was tied up with her mouth taped shut and the gunman was pointing his weapon at her. I saw MJ asleep in his playpen behind them.

Tears began to form in my eyes but I held them in. I couldn't afford to be weak right now. The man wanted something from me and I needed to go along with whatever it was to ensure my family's safety.

I looked the man dead in the eyes and said, "Like I said who are you and what do you want?"

"Let's not get into the details here sweetheart. Come with me, if you want them to stay alive."

He didn't say another word as he turned around and headed out the hotel exit. I followed right behind his ass thinking about all the ways I was gonna kill his ass for the shit he was doing. He stopped once we got to the curb in front of a black van. He pulled the door back and that's when that bitch Carina came into view.

Before I knew what was happening the man shoved me forward into the van. I held onto my stomach to shield my unborn from the fall. Carina stood over me on the floor of the vehicle and kicked me in the face. I faded out of consciousness praying to God

Messiah got to his mother and our son before anything happened.

To be continued...

Made in United States
Orlando, FL
30 September 2024